ANGELA *of the* STONES

BARACOA

ANGELA *of the* STONES

stories by

AMANDA HALE

thistledown press

Thistledown Press Ltd.
410 2nd Avenue North
Saskatoon, Saskatchewan, S7K 2C3
www.thistledownpress.com

Library and Archives Canada Cataloguing in Publication
Hale, Amanda, author
Angela of the stones / Amanda Hale.
Short stories.
Issued in print and electronic formats.
ISBN 978-1-77187-165-5 (softcover).–ISBN 978-1-77187-166-2 (HTML).–ISBN 978-1-77187-167-9 (PDF)
I. Title.
PS8565.A4313A64 2018   C813'.6   C2018-904563-9
C2018-904564-7

Cover and book design by Jackie Forrie
Printed and bound in Canada
Author photo by Kim June Johnson

Canada

Canada Council
for the Arts

Conseil des Arts
du Canada

ARTS BOARD

cultivating
the arts

Thistledown Press gratefully acknowledges the financial assistance of the Canada Council for the Arts, the Saskatchewan Arts Board, and the Government of Canada for its publishing program.

ACKNOWLEDGEMENTS

Most of my research for these stories has been done on the streets of Baracoa, and a portion on Calle Ocho, the Little Havana neighborhood of Miami. Thanks to all the generous Cuban friends who have responded to my questions, discussing with me over kitchen tables and on park benches, the extraordinary and unique country in which you live. This is your book; you are the source and inspiration, I am merely the scribe.

Thank you to Thistledown Press for your ongoing loyalty to my writing; and to Seán Virgo, for your brilliant and exacting editorial guidance.

Gracias to 'my man in Havana,' Tomás Aquilino López Sánchez, who is always ready to respond to my e-mail queries; and to Manuel García Verdecia, my friend and translator.

to the people of Baracoa who have so generously shared with me their memories, dreams and reflections during many years of friendship

CONTENTS

'Ah, the power of silence,' the painter says, leaning back. 'What is he thinking?'

'Perhaps he's remembering all the words he's said for all these years. He's earned his silence,' the peanut vendor says.

And in the silence that follows, as Romero ponders his friend's reply, Godo imagines Fidel lying in an old man's bed, narrow, monkish, raising a trembling finger as he opens his mouth to speak.

A church has stood in the centre of Baracoa for more than five hundred years. When the Spanish anchored off the shores of Playa Caribe in late November of 1492, they marveled at the beauty of a Taíno Indian village clasped by a fist of rivers flowing from densely treed mountains to the confluence of Atlantic and Caribbean oceans. They saw the long tabletop mountain of El Yunque emerging from the jungle in the distance, haloed by a puff of cloud reflected in the calm waters surrounding them. Captain Cristóbal Colón first imprinted with his own bare foot the damp white sands of the bay, then he planted a wooden cross there, plunging it deep as he named the bay Porto Santo. He wrote later in his ship's logbook that it was 'the most beautiful place in the world with its fresh breezes and crystal clear water . . . I hear the birds singing that they will never ever leave this place.'

Aurelia gazes up at the newly renovated church. La Catedral de Nuestra Señora de la Asunción had become a crumbling white bone until the recent two years of restorations, with carpenters, painters and stonemasons crawling all over the structure, hammering and chiselling, shouting back and forth, singing as they worked. Now it stands empty, the new concrete bell towers freshly painted for el Quinto Centenario de Baracoa, la Ciudad Primada. A full moon of a clock has been donated by the Italian city of Bergamo, and when it tolls the hour all the citizens of Baracoa, wherever they happen to be, are reminded of the beating heart of their church, so long under renovation.

'And all for nothing,' Aurelia sighs, because Padre Luigi has been sent away.

When she first saw him, loping down the side aisle of the church, his long hair flying, his slight body draped in a white cassock, Aurelia had been reminded of the picture in her Bible that showed Jesus Christ with his disciples at the miracle of the loaves and fishes. Padre Luigi could have been any one of them but, with his bright eyes and beaked nose, he especially resembled Christ. She would see him on the street, striding along, though never in a hurry, always taking time to stop and talk, his head to one side as he fingered his beard with quick nervous gestures. He seemed to Aurelia a walking contradiction — a man in perpetual motion even when he stood still, energy crackling around him as he listened patiently, his deep-set eyes brimming with compassion.

Padre Mauricio, who has been sent from Guantánamo to replace Luigi, stands at the open door of the church watching a few sad souls slouched on the benches in Parque Central, hugging the shade as the sun swirls blindly towards its mid-day zenith. The streets are empty. The church is empty. It reminds him of the dark days when Church properties had been nationalized and the faithful forced underground. So broad had been the 1960s sweep that even the Jesuit school where the Castro brothers had attended was closed, forcing the priests to pack up and move to Miami. Mauricio scans the street again, frowns and runs a broad hand over his shining pate as he checks his watch — nine-fifteen. He turns on his heel, walks up the aisle and kneels stiffly to pray for continence. But his anger will not be quelled. When he hears a click behind him and turns to see a tourist with her camera pointed at the new stained-glass windows above the altar, he shouts, '*¡La iglesia está cerrada!*' and, rising painfully, he shuffles out the side door to the refuge of his new lodgings in the Casa Paroquial.

On his last night in Baracoa Padre Luigi had hosted an evening of music for the youth of his parish. Los Huracanes, a local band, played old favourites from the sixties — "A Whiter Shade of Pale," and "Stand by Me." People had lined up to recite poems they'd written for Luigi, to thank him and bid him farewell. The parish house had been packed to the rafters and Aurelia had been there too, mixing in with the young ones. In all those years she had never spoken directly with the padre. She was a shy woman who stood on the sidelines, but this night she knew was her last chance, and even though she felt unworthy, Aurelia found herself swept forward with a throng of boys and girls clamoring to bid Luigi a personal farewell. She stared at him as though she might capture him in her mind forever. So concentrated was her gaze that when she found herself face to face with him she could hardly believe it, and she blurted out her question without thinking — 'Where are you going?' She'd heard a rumour that he was being sent to the church of Caridad del Cobre near Santiago de Cuba. At least he'll still be in Cuba, she'd thought, only five hours away.

'Back to Italy, to my birthplace,' he said sadly. 'Bergamo.'

Aurelia's face must have spoken all that she felt, because Padre Luigi embraced her and for a moment their two hearts reached for each other, beating from inside their bony cages. When he pulled back she saw the tears she'd felt when her cheek had pressed against his.

Sundays in Baracoa are distinct from all the other days. Shops are closed, people sleep late, even the peanut vendor doesn't hit the streets until afternoon. The faithful congregate in their various churches — Catholic, Baptist, Pentecostal, Seventh Day Adventist — then the women go home to their laundry and house-cleaning, to cook a meal and gather round the table with family. But since Luigi's departure not one of the Catholic congregation has ventured forth. Padre Mauricio is fuming. Behind his anger is a snarling animal fearful for its survival. What will he tell the Archbishop? What about the collection money? How about his sermons piling up undelivered? He's been door to door, sweating in the summer heat, his hatless dome burning.

'Why were you not in church last Sunday?'

'*Mi hija está muy enferma, Padre.* I have to take care of her.'

'I was away in Moa. My work takes me there every weekend.'

'*Me lastimé la pierna.* The doctor says I mustn't walk until it's better.'

The excuses are endless. No-one has actually said the word, but Padre Mauricio knows he is dealing with *una huelga* — a silent passive strike at the heart of Nuestra Señora de la Asunción. His congregation is protesting against the expulsion of their beloved Luigi, and there isn't a damn thing he can do about it short of recalling the banished *Italianito!*

Last year Aurelia travelled all the way from Baracoa to La Cuchilla to witness the baptism of her great-niece. A swollen stream bubbled through the village and children had been playing there, splashing each other and laughing as a dog barked from the other side of the stream and plunged in, almost drowning in his effort to reach the children. Aurelia watched a litter of piglets rooting in the bushes, unburdened as yet by their fleshy destiny. She had just joined the women gathered around the new mother and her baby daughter when Padre Luigi arrived and began distributing clothing and food to the *campesinos.*

'We will have a distribution of shoes,' he'd said, 'as soon as they arrive from La Habana, and there will be water tanks installed in each hamlet, to catch rain water for you to siphon into your jugs — fresh clean drinking water.'

The children had tried on their new T-shirts — SEREMOS COMO EL CHE, emblazoned on this latest consignment, with a dark outline of the Argentinian hero against a pale blue sky.

When the *padrino* and *madrina* had arrived in an ox-drawn cart, rumbling down the muddy road, everyone gathered in a circle and began to sing. As Aurelia watched Padre Luigi standing under a burgeoning mango tree dressed in his white cassock, arms spread, singing lustily, she'd felt a swell of emotion. She couldn't get out of her mind that image of Christ in the desert, feeding the multitude with only five barley loaves and two small fish, and she had for the first time been inspired to ponder the metaphoric nature of the Bible.

When the hymn was over someone had brought a small dish of water, and Luigi had dipped his thumb and tenderly pressed it to the forehead of the sleeping infant, making the sign of the cross while the *madrina* and *padrino* made their vows as godparents to watch over the child and guide her.

Luigi's discourse had focused on the coming celebration of the 500th anniversary, and specifically on the *Cruz de la Parra* and the symbolism of that crucifix which had endured since the days of Cristóbal Colón. Aurelia wondered how this Italian had grown to be more Cuban than the Cubans. From where did his passion come, and why did it affect her so?

Padre Mauricio disembarks at the Guantánamo terminal, pushes his way through the slow crowd, and hails a taxi. He has been preoccupied throughout the three-hour journey with the knotty problem of his congregation and their ill-founded political action. This silent rebellion has come as a surprise from a people whose religious freedom was suspended for so many years. Only in '92 had Fidel dropped the government's atheist stance and begun to release religious believers from labour camps. Ah, and then had come the unforgettable visit of His Holiness in January '98 — *'Inolvidable,'* Mauricio sighs as he remembers that joyous revival of Catholicism. Politics has no place in the spiritual life, he tells himself, beginning to formulate in his mind a sermon on the topic. As the shepherd of his flock Mauricio feels responsible for their spiritual welfare, and this weighs heavily on him as his taxi speeds towards the Archbishop's residence.

Once admitted to the marble-columned edifice he is kept waiting an uncomfortable length of time, but he swallows the anger that rises in his gorge, along with the rumbling hunger in his gut. He crosses and re-crosses his aching legs. His calves are knotted with varicose veins — all these years of standing at the altar of the Lord. Finally the secretary ushers him into the presence of the Archbishop, who is resting after his lunch and greets Mauricio with a gracious smile and gestures for him to sit.

Mauricio hands over his written report which may never be read judging by the dismissive gesture with which it is received. But the Archbishop does seem genuinely concerned. He raises a soft-voiced inquiry into the question of the collection money. The Baracoan congregation has never caused concern in the past. What seems to be the problem? When the padre voices his suspicions about *la huelga* the Archbishop smiles and waves his ringed hand as though swatting a fly, but a frown creases his brow at the suggestion of reinstating Padre Luigi. 'Impossible,' he says gently. 'We must move forward with confidence in the new order.' He will speak with the officials of Poder Popular Baracoa, the Municipal Government body. Mauricio is urged to return immediately to Baracoa and await further instructions.

There is no bus till tomorrow. He has to travel in a cattle truck, crammed in with a bunch of *campesinos*, standing all the way. His varicose veins plague him.

Everyone remembers the panic last year when the authorities issued a tsunami warning; and even though the tsunami
had not manifested as the gigantic wave they had run from
in fear, the citizens of Baracoa had suffered it emotionally as
though it had really happened. While everyone fled to high
ground with babes in arms and small dogs clasped to their
breast, Luigi had run back and forth, helping the elderly and
infirm onto the street and up to the safety of El Castillo, or
to the neighbourhood of El Paraíso which also stood on high
ground — numerous trips, mindless of his own safety. Aurelia
had seen him coming and going from her perch on the wall
of El Castillo, and she had wanted to join him, but was afraid
for her life and had felt cowardly and ashamed when the
all-clear sounded and the people were instructed to return
to their homes. The dignitaries of Poder Popular had run for
safety too without a thought for the people they served — the
hospital and hotel staff likewise, and the padres and pastors
of the various churches. Aurelia was not alone. But she had
resolved to be more like Padre Luigi, though this seemed
arrogant and somewhat disrespectful of his person, but it was
in truth her heart's desire.

The Archbishop of Guantánamo meets with the officials of
Poder Popular to discuss the difficult question of his Baracoan
congregation. When he shows them Padre Mauricio's report
they break into a cacophony of protest.

'*Una huelga? Ridículo!* Never heard of such a thing.
Especially not in Baracoa.'

'La Habana is a different matter. Those Habaneros can be
rebellious. But Baracoa . . . ?'

'You must go there, Seigneur, and speak to them.'

After the Archbishop has persuaded them of the unlike-lihood of his congregation gathering to listen to him — this indeed being the crux of the matter — he presents his plan to the esteemed *compañeros*.

And so it is that a group of specialists travel undercover from Guantánamo to Baracoa carrying tourist backpacks filled with electronic equipment. They move furtively from house to house, guided by Padre Mauricio who has compiled a list of the more suspect members of his congregation. They work next door to the Catholic families, but where possible in their very houses, where they install hidden microphones and recording equipment linked to a central office in Poder Popular which has no choice but to cooperate with the Archdiocese of Guantánamo. Once the equipment is in place Mauricio retires to the Casa Paroquial. It is no longer in his hands. He begins to wash himself assiduously until his skin begins to dry out, cracking and flaking uncomfortably.

On a stifling August Monday the people of Baracoa had gathered at the Plaza de la Revolución in La Punta overlooking La Bahia where a port thrived until the fall of the USSR twenty years earlier. Aurelia was jostled by the crowd, but she held her ground in fervent anticipation of the Mass which was to follow the speeches made by the mayor and by other prominent members of local government; by the Historian of Baracoa freshly returned from a trip to Spain where he has solicited funds for yet another of his many projects, by the first secretary of the Communist Party, by the director of the Casa de Cultura, and so on, until finally — oh finally, Aurelia's shoulders rose as she clasped her hands together — Padre Luigi with his quick step was crossing the Plaza in a fresh white cassock, something held tightly in his hand. Perhaps his speech, she thought, but no, when Luigi mounted the dais he quickly unfurled the white scarf he had held, and bound his own mouth with it. There he stood, gagged, and suddenly everyone understood — the Archbishop had forbidden him to speak. He performed the Mass like that, his tortured brown eyes expressing all his feelings as each member of the congregation stood before him to take the host on their tongue, sharing with Luigi and with each other the clamour of a profound and eloquent silence.

Luigi had spoken out about the plight of Baracoa, about the irony of the city being lauded for its history yet receiving little more than a coat of paint in prominent places to impress the visiting dignitaries on the day of the anniversary. He had spoken out against the poverty that afflicted Baracoa and its surrounding countryside because the provincial government in Guantánamo took the lion's share and tossed only the leftovers at Baracoa. Luigi had spoken out in appreciation of his congregation, which had swelled dramatically during his five years in office. He had become dangerous and so he had received, by special courier, from the Archbishop's office in Guantánamo, official notice of his expulsion. The cost of the courier service alone would have provided food for an entire family for a week.

Forbidden to speak at the Mass, the little Italian padre published his intended speech in the monthly church bulletin under the title 'La marginación de la primera ciudad de Cuba.' When Aurelia read it her resolve to emulate Luigi surged. She had begun to write messages to herself in the privacy of her room in the small house she shared with her two widowed sisters on Calle Primero de Abril. She had printed on scraps of paper — *SEREMOS COMO EL CHE* — so that, if they were found, her secret desire, to be not like Che but like Padre Luigi, would not be revealed. She had placed the reminders around her room — under her pillow, on the windowsill, on her dresser, between the pages of her Bible. The bulletin with Padre Luigi's speech she placed carefully in the drawer of her dresser, where she stood each night to read it in front of her mirror before she slept, plumping her resolve.

Aurelia listened more carefully to her sisters' complaints about their failing health. She bought extra tomatoes and gave them to her neighbour Yolanda who rarely got out since she'd developed diabetes. She smiled more readily and felt a quickening in her step. Every day Aurelia wrote another note and smiled to herself with growing self-respect.

'Gimme a *Criollo*,' Yoel says, turning to his *compañero*.

Yurubí jerks awake and puts a cigarette between his own lips before flipping the crumpled packet at his workmate. He reaches into his pocket for a match. He has none, neither does Yoel. They stare at each other, shrug, and return to their headsets. They've sat through weeks of numbing silence broken only by the clatter of pots and pans as lunchtime approaches, and on Sundays the *whirr* and *swish* of a washing machine or the slap of cloth on stone from a backyard patio.

Yoel's body tenses as he catches the sound of soft voices under the click of cutlery. This latter makes his mouth water, filling his mind with images of plates loaded with food, like the slide projections on the wall of the Hotel Habanero on

Saturday nights. Yoel's wife has hung propaganda posters in their kitchen, but the food she serves bears no resemblance to the meats, vegetables and salads glistening with oil and drops of vinegar that loom before him. He strains to hear what the rebellious Catholics are saying — a word, just one word is all he needs — *Huelga!* — but there's nothing now but a low hum broken by intermittent crackling. If only he had a match to light his cigarette, then his stomach might stop growling.

'*¡Coño!* ¿Qué estamos haciendo aquí?' he says, slamming down his headset.

Yurubí shrugs. 'It's a job. We're not paid to ask questions.'

'What if we told them we heard something?'

'Whaddya mean?'

'A word. You know. Strike!'

'But I never heard . . . '

'I'm not talking about what you heard, *imbécil!* I'm talking about using our imagination, putting an end to this fucking tedious job.'

'*¡No puedo, no puedo! Soy hombre honesto,*' Yurubí protests.

'Agh, come on, just a little white lie, *compañero.* People hear things all the time.'

'No!' Yurubí slams his fist on the table, upsetting the transmitter and disconnecting the fragile wires.

'*¡Aiee coño! ¿Hermano, qué haces?*'

'Gimme five pesos,' Yurubí demands. 'I'll go buy sandwiches while you fix this.'

As Padre Luigi had boarded the morning bus to Santiago his heart was filled with the previous night's farewells, the music of Los Huracanes pulsing still in his veins, the sad eyes of

Aurelia Fernandez Pérez haunting him. From Santiago he was to fly to La Habana where he would connect four hours later with a direct flight to Milano, close enough to his hometown. It had all been arranged by the Archbishop's office, the tickets booked, paid for, and delivered by special courier to the Casa Paroquial in Baracoa.

As the bus had rumbled along the Malecón, belching black smoke, Luigi pondered the irony of his situation so he did not at first realize what was happening. The bus slowed and came to a sudden jerking halt. Necks craned down the aisle and one or two brave souls jumped up to see what was going on. It was only when Luigi heard his name being chanted over and over that he stood up and walked to the front of the bus. They were at the corner of the Matachín Museum where the Historian of Baracoa presided over his dusty colonial relics. Ahead of them was the looming concrete statue of Cristóbal Colón. Their way was blocked by a crowd of teenagers chanting, 'Padre Luigi, Padre Luigi!'

He had stared in disbelief, then slowly his mouth spread in a huge grin as he read the crudely scrawled posters that the children held up — TE AMAMOS PADRE LUIGI — POR FAVOR REGRESA PRONTO — SIEMPRE TE RECORDAREMOS . . . We love you Padre Luigi — please come back soon — we will always remember you . . .

It was a full ten minutes before the bus driver was able to get through. Only when he threatened to call the police had the young folk of Baracoa begun to disperse, sad but triumphant. As they waved goodbye to Padre Luigi, he noticed that many of them were wearing their *SEREMOS COMO EL CHE* T-shirts.

∾∾∾∾

ÁNGELA DE LAS PIEDRAS

Midnight. Ángela counts the chimes of the full moon clock floating above her. She sees it dimly through the film of cloth that covers her from head to toe, clinging to the skin of her face where it quivers with each breath. She's stashed her sack of tin cans and bottles under her bench. It takes all day to collect them from tourists slurping their beer, rum, *refrescos*, tossing the cans away. She's helped the old man again. People say he's her father, but he is not. Only that he lives free like her, sleeping outside like a dog curled in on himself. Where does he sleep? On the beach, with his own sack of garbage? Ángela has Parque Central to herself, but she has to wait till everyone's gone home and all the tourists have stumbled back to their *casas* and their comfortable beds. Godofredo leaves soon as the bars close because he has somewhere to go. He shares a house with his sister — Casa Maní, they call it, because he is the peanut vendor. '¡*Maní, maní!*' Whenever Ángela hears him calling she runs to get her peanuts. He always gives her an extra cone for free, and a nice smile. Eugenia has gone too — she leaves early with the remains of her chocolate bars and *cucuruchu*. She lives on Playa Caribe by the stadium. She collects wood

22

from the beach and lights a fire in the night to cook her fish and vegetables, then she sleeps by the embers listening to the waves crashing on the sand. She is the happiest person Ángela knows. Every day the same blouse, the same skirt, but it's her face that people see with that big smile and her teeth shining white like new grave-stones. She asks the tourists for their clothes and they laugh at her, but Eugenia doesn't care. One day a tourist gave her a red blouse. That's the one she wears, every day, every month, every year. The years do pass, Ángela knows. Now it's a new one, *año nuevo*, another anniversary of the Revolution has passed. Last year was the lost year. They took her to the hospital in Guantánamo because she was angry with the tourists who stared at her, shooting with their cameras, shooting shooting, without her permission. 'I am the President of Baracoa!', she had shouted. 'You have no right!' They took her away over a steep winding road and forced her to sleep against her will, a long dark time.

Ángela turns slowly on the hard bench, easing her sore hip out from under. She fits perfectly. She is short, but her arms and legs are strong. Her scalp itches suddenly beneath her tangle of hair and she scratches furiously at it, digging with stubby fingers. She has a gap-toothed comb she found on the street, purple with long fat teeth — must have dropped from a tourist's backpack, they don't have combs like that in Cuba. On Sunday mornings she holds it above her head like a magic wand and pulls it through her hair blessing herself with the strange words she has heard coming from their mouths . . . 'ee mael . . . deena . . . kees' . . . Sometimes the Sisters take her in and give her a shower, scrub her skin until it shines like burnished guayacán. Sister Magdalena washes her hair, but her hands are

23

rough and Ángela winces as her hair is pulled this way and that, but afterwards she feels good, wrapped in a towel like a little girl, her skin pink and tingling. She's forgotten how old she is, though she does remember those birthdays when Mami made cake and *ensalada fria*. She hasn't seen Mami for such a long time. They've all disappeared, the people she remembers. No-one came to see her in the hospital. But she's home now and she will visit Mami . . . in the cemetery on the hill . . . high above Baracoa . . . drifting, drifting, a warm comfortable feeling . . . legs twitching under her shroud . . . drifting into the church under the full moon clock. She must be late because the church is already full. Ángela stands at the door and watches. The people rise and sing, then they sit and listen, they kneel and bow their heads with closed eyes. Ángela marches up the centre aisle and stands before the altar staring at the bald padre with the shining head as he swings his censer. She breathes in the sweet pungent smoke. She wants more so she reaches for her pipe with the stub of tobacco sticking out of the bowl, searches in her pockets, can't find matches. A firm hand grips her arm and she swings around ready to fight, but it's only Sister Magdalena urging her into the Sisters' pew in the seat at the end so she can see. Ángela's face creases into a smile as she sits, her back curved in prayer, flaring into the roundness of a bottom that gives her ballast and fills the material of her shorts — not the tight *calenticos* that the *jineteras* wear — longer, more like a skirt. Ángela has a deep sense of modesty and when the young men in Parque Central taunt her with filthy comments about her body she screams at them, her fist slapping into her palm.

She wakes suddenly, hands clasped, her breath rapid and shallow. But no-one is there. It's only the memory of that day when she lost herself, heard nothing but the screeching of her own voice, louder and louder, blocking out their cruel words. She'd scurried back and forth, unable to leave them be, and suddenly she'd found herself bent double over the roots of the giant mango in the middle of Parque Central, scrabbling for a stone. She'd found one, small but sharp-edged, and hauled back with her right arm ready to pitch it. Then one of the men darted over. 'No, no!' he'd shouted, wagging his finger at her. 'Don't you throw stones at me. Drop the stone, drop it!' '*¡Angela de las piedras!*' shouts another one, jeering at her, and they all join in — '*¡Ángela de las piedras, de las piedras, de las piedras!*' Ángela trembles as sweat breaks out on her itching scalp. She feels the stone still clenched in her palm, remembers that night on the beach when they'd found her sleeping in the bushes and rammed their things into her, bouncing her on the hard sand. A fresh wave of anger rises. She's lost her stone. She has no defence but her voice. The men cluster with their backs to her and she can feel the eyes of everyone in the park staring at her, but she doesn't care. Her fury is a red tide rising with nowhere to go. She runs through the park screaming until she finds herself in front of the Casa Paroquial calling out for Padre Luigi who has blessed her and given her communion at Sunday Mass. She calls and calls, her eyes closed as she has seen the parishioners' eyes closed in prayer. Where is Padre Luigi? Her throat aches with unshed tears. He would have given her refuge, but they've sent him away. 'I am the President of Baracoa! I am a person of importance! I will not bear these insults!' She remembers a hand on her shoulder as she turns again, restless on her bench — the smooth face of a turbaned woman hovering above her outside the Casa Paroquial. 'Ángela,' she had said quietly, 'Come, my dear, I am your friend Delfina. Let us go to *Casa Chocolate* and eat *helados*. *Estás invitado*.' Delfina had placed her arm lightly upon Ángela's shoulders and suddenly all her fury had drained away, splashing around her ankles like rain. Her arms dropped to her sides and she went quietly with Delfina, a few people still staring as they walked away from the park, crossed the cobbled square in front of the Municipal Offices of Poder Popular, walking towards the Boulevard as though it were a normal day — two friends taking a stroll. The men have forgotten her. To them she is like a dog to be baited at the Sunday fights in Playita where they whip their animals into a fury and set them on each other.

The clock strikes one. Ángela is motionless except for the faint rise and fall of her covering. How can it turn from twelve to one so quickly? She has seen the waxing of the moon, a gradual thing, night after night until it is a golden ball, round as the new church clock. It has been sent, they say, all the way from Padre Luigi's birthplace. She sees it glimmering through the film of her cloth and she feels safe. He has sent the clock to watch over her. If I had found a stone on the beach that night, she thinks, I would have pounded their heads until they no longer moved. She remembers the men as one creature with many limbs and heads, like a monster risen from the sea. After the attack she'd stopped sleeping on the beach and lay down instead under the flickering lamps of the dimly lit park. But she had not slept for many nights afterwards. Too frightened to close her eyes, she'd lain shrouded, motionless, as the scene played over and over in her mind, blasting tunnels of fury into her brain.

Ángela knows everyone in Baracoa. She's sat in the classroom alongside fifty *compañeritos*, she's worked at the *pizzería* washing dishes with the other staff, she goes to church every Sunday, she knows them all. But she has not told anyone what happened to her, not even Delfina or Sister Magdalena. Especially not the Sisters. Who would listen to a girl who's been in the hospital in Guantánamo? 'Am I to blame?' she whispers. 'Is there something about me that frightens people, something that makes men attack me in the night?' She remembers from school the words of José Martí — *Patria es humanidad*. Ángela smiles as she holds the echo of that word in her mouth — *humanidad*. A good word. A secret. When daylight comes I will be safe, she thinks. I will lift another stone and raise my voice to God.

27

J uly 2012

'My name is Gertrudis. I have lived in Santiago de Cuba all my life. I was twenty-two years old when the revolutionaries attacked the Moncada Barracks. They came to our hospital — the Saturnino Lora Military Hospital behind the Barracks. They were led by Abel Santamaria. Another group attacked the Palacio de Justicia, and they were led by Raúl Castro who was a young man then. Now he is eighty-one years old, like me, and he talks of stepping down from the Presidency of Cuba at the end of his next term.' Gertrudis leans forward in her cane-seated *balánce* and fixes her visitor with all the intensity of her cloudy brown eyes.

'I was working on the early morning shift and I saw them burst in, running down the corridor — Abel, his sister Haydée, Melba Hernandez right behind her, and the others tumbling after. It was as though they were an avalanche of stones and pebbles rolling to earth. I saw how terrified they were as they ran past me, and it made me afraid of what was to happen. I was newly graduated as a nurse, and six months married to Ramón. We had made love that morning, in the half light as dawn was gathering to break. I was full of him still — my Ramón with his big square hands all over my body, his soft lips pressed on mine, becoming hard and insistent as he entered me.'

The visitor drops his eyes and studies the floor, embarrassed by her frankness.

'No, that's not what you want to hear,' Gertrudis says, smiling to herself as she crosses the room, her gait slow and arthritic. She enters the kitchen and pours two cups of strong coffee from the freshly brewed pot, adding generous spoonfuls of sugar, stirring.

'*Moncada: Siembra Gloriosa; Siempre es 26 — primer impulso; 26 de Julio, Batalla de las Ideas; Un Mundo Mejor es Posible,*' she recites loudly on her journey back to the *sala*. 'Signs all over the countryside surrounding Santiago de Cuba, on the highway to Guantánamo, to Baracoa, and probably all the way to La Habana.'

The visitor observes her knotted fingers as she places a coffee cup in his hands. He looks up into her face, nodding a thank you. She is a handsome woman with the kind of beauty that endures until the end because it rests on good bones and a good heart. He watches her trundle across the *sala*, the little cup rattling in its saucer as she places it carefully on the table beside her rocker.

'I have never been to La Habana. I am a Santiaguera, born in Oriente, in this cradle of the Revolution.' She sinks heavily in the chair, setting it in motion. '*26 de Julio siempre* — always, always that day echoing through our nation, fifty-nine years past, another anniversary coming up, and must I speak yet again, to give my testimony of that dreadful day at the hospital? *Siempre, siempre,* always on my mind, shaping my thoughts. Will you never let me forget?'

He raises a hand as though to stop her, but Gertrudis continues with a sweep of her arm. 'The rebels demanded patients' uniforms. I stood against the wall while our ward sister delved into the laundry hampers to find enough gowns and bandages until we had them all outfitted, lying in beds and on trestles. For that day we turned our hospital into a refuge. We stopped caring for the sick and harboured the revolutionaries, pretending to care for them as they pretended to be patients. It was Sister herself who denounced them. I was watching her face. I'd seen the conflict raging inside her, the pain in her expression as she said, Yes, yes, they are here, in that bed, and that one, and that one. I am a Seventh Day Adventist. I am forbidden to lie. Please do not harm them. This is a hospital, a place of healing.'

Gertrudis shakes her head, her steel-grey hair stiff, hardly moving on her brown scalp. He detects liver spots on her hands, but her cheek is smooth, almost like that of a girl, he thinks. Because she is plump and will never have the withered, scrawny look of some old women.

'Batista's men dragged them one by one, ripping the pyjamas and bandages off them. They were silent, so silent as they were taken away. And we were silent too until they were gone from our hospital, and then we broke into excited chatter. Some of us were weeping. We didn't know why. We didn't know what it was about, then one of the girls said, it's the rebels, Fidel Castro and his followers. Pappy talks about them. He says they're trying to save Cuba from Batista.'

I, Gertrudis

She leans back in her rocking hair, setting it in motion. 'My name is Gertrudis and this is my testimony.'

Sunlight spills through the open door, changing the hue of the polished cement floor, shooting it through with all the brilliant colour of crushed stone. 'Three generations of entries and exits have touched this spot,' she says with a smile. 'I was born in this house and I'm going to be eighty-two — four years younger than Fidel. He was almost twenty-six years old on that day — 26th of July, 1953, the first assault in a revolution that took six and a half years to triumph. He's an old war horse, and I have my memories too, though I have lost them with this constant repetition. Why don't you leave me in peace?'

The man tenses, ready to rise.

'No, no.' Gertrudis shakes her finger at him. 'I will tell you. Otherwise how will you know the truth of it.'

He nods and leans back, hands resting on his thighs.

'I didn't see any of them again after the soldiers dragged them away. But of course I did, because what happened to them has played over and over in my head, screams spinning around my skull clamouring for escape. Did Abel scream as they gouged out his eyes? Did Boris scream when they cut off his testicles? They say that Haydee would not give them the satisfaction of her tears when they brought her brother's eyes on a plate, when they rubbed her fiancé's warm testicles on her face. I am numb as I speak these words. It was all so long ago and now indeed we have a different world, but is it better? We lived well under the Russians, with enough food, everything cheap and plentiful. People say it was fine until that bitter period when the Soviet Union fell and we were starving, scraping the skins of *platanos* and grinding them down to make gruel for our children, washing our clothes with stones, rubbing them threadbare. Now my life is easier. I am old and hunger does not plague me in the same way. I appreciate every mouthful.

'The real change began in 1980 when Celia Sánchez died and Fidel was left to govern alone. Celia was our Queen. Fidel would not move on anything without her approval. It was she who prepared the way for the triumph of the Revolution. Celia was enraged when a child she had known from birth was raped to death by American gangsters in La Habana. It was her anger that was the true seed of our Revolution.'

Gertrudis pauses and leans forward again, her voice dropping as her brown eyes sparkle through their cloudiness. 'The Moncada fortress was only 850 metres from the Colegio de Dolores, the Jesuit-run school attended by the Castro boys. They knew every alley, while the young rebels,' she shrugs, 'they were orphans and *campesinos* who didn't know the city. It was easy for Batista's men to chase them down. But Fidel ducked into a safe house, then he was transferred to another and by afternoon he was in the countryside. Raúl remained hidden in the city.' Gertrudis smooths her skirt over ample thighs, her head nodding sideways as though weighing the odds. 'Not many people know this. It will be our secret,' she cautions with a direct look at her visitor before she continues. 'Fidel's time among the elite served him well. The Colegio de Dolores was patronized by rich Catholic families, and Fidel's older brother persuaded the Rector of the college to pressure the authorities with strict instructions to take Fidel alive. As you know, he was arrested, tried, and sent to prison. That's when Celia began an exchange of letters with Fidel in his prison cell on Isla de Pinos. Together they plotted, but she *did* it all, she assembled an army of women in the Sierra Maestra and laid the groundwork while Fidel was released and exiled to Mexico where he met Che Guevara and gathered his band of men to voyage home to Cuba in the Granma, a yacht purchased in Mexico through a rich contact. When Fidel and Che arrived Celia was ready with everything they needed.'

The visitor is desperate to write it all down, but he dares not break the spell. His eyes are riveted on Gertrudis' face as he tries to remember her every word.

'Celia is our well-kept secret. Fidel will not speak of her. He harbours her memory jealously, and if you ask him he will raise his hands, palms out, like a man surrendering to a firing squad, his long fingers bent and tremulous, filled with the memory of her hands, her face, her sweet smile.'

Her eyes close for a few seconds and she rocks, a calmness coming over her. 'The hospital is a museum now,' she declaims, 'And here we stand for our annual memorial, in this front hall where photographs of Abel and his *compañeros* hang, reminding us of their terrible deaths. This is what I usually say, my friend,' she drops her voice in an aside. 'Haydee and Melba were spared. They served only a short term in prison, because it couldn't be proven that they had carried weapons. Haydee remained loyal to Fidel until her suicide on July 26, 1980, the same year that Celia died. Was she unable to deny any longer that the Moncada attack had been the foolish idea of a privileged young man playing terrorist, and that Celia's battle, fought from a well-organized base in the mountains, had been better thought out? No, you don't want to hear that either. And your *compañeros,* they definitely don't want to

33

hear it.' She laughs so heartily and so long that he has to join her, although he is uncomfortable with his own laughter. It has a false ring in his ears.

Gertrudis dabs her eyes with a handkerchief and nods to the visitor before she resumes. 'All of Cuba is a museum now. That's what the tourists want, to see the relics of our Revolution — the tanks put out to grass behind the Museum in La Habana, the yacht that brought our exiled revolutionaries back from Mexico listing as they file past, peering in the windows, looking for the ghosts of men who died in an ambush trying to reach the place where Celia was waiting with jeeps, guns, gasoline. We live off our old Revolution, but how much longer can it continue? Soon there will be no-one alive who remembers it. I will be eighty-two, Fidel will be eighty-six. My son lives in Miami, my daughter in Spain, two of my grandchildren have gone to Ecuador. My story has lost its meaning and in the annual repetition of it I have lost my true memories. Sometimes I catch myself in a moment of reawakening to the true horror of what happened. And that I, Gertrudis Moreno Escobar, an ordinary girl, a young nurse, should brush up against people like them. Who were they? I remember Frank País, twenty-two years old like me, his mami telling him to be careful as he left her house for the last time. She had no idea what he was doing, how dangerous it was, and what would happen to him, her young son, her baby, his life cut short. Fidel surrounded himself with young people, many of them fatherless and poor, and very few negroes. They were loyal to Batista because of his mixed blood.'

Gertrudis heaves herself up from the rocking chair, surprisingly agile for a large old woman, and shuffles towards the kitchen, but when she reaches it she merely plunks her cup down on the counter, turns again and stares at the wall as though she's forgotten what she came for. Ah, she's forgotten to remove *his* cup.

'I go off down blind alleys,' she mumbles to herself, plodding back to the *sala*. 'As I tell my story unseen roads open,' she says firmly, 'Like newly formed coronary arteries developing with exercise. The body and mind have great abilities to heal and grow in the most unexpected directions, you know. I, Gertrudis tell my story from a distance of fifty-nine years, and it is just that, a story, but in the telling I begin to understand what it has meant, and how it has led us to where we are now — trapped in our own blind alley — but at least I can look back and see how I got here.'

She sits heavily, setting the *balánce* in such vigorous motion that her feet are lifted off the ground with the first couple of swings.

'No, no,' she cautions herself. 'You will want me to repeat what I've always said. But I tell you, *compañero*, I am afraid of what I might say this year, because when the truth comes it is irresistible. I am afraid of falling away, lulled by the heat and the midday sun, seduced by my own body into a dream world where Ramón awaits me, and where it all becomes clear finally. How will I resist that? Abel smiling with shining eyes, Boris cupping his testicles, heavy and full between his legs, and Haydee with him finally, by his side. No, you don't want to hear this. You want me to listen, to sit upright and nod in agreement. You want us all to listen to your speeches, give our testimony, and then march. When I was a child I had trouble distinguishing between the meaning of compulsory and

35

voluntary — I would define those words for myself each time I used them, to check that I was correct. But I have learned the meaning of compulsory in a most visceral manner, for it has been our life here in Cuba. Voluntary is for me only a word. My body does not understand it, but oh how my soul clamours for it.'

She drops her head and ruminates a few moments, then looks up at him laughing softly to herself. 'Yes, of course. My daughter Darvis is coming with the grandchildren and we will sit and rock and talk, though I have less and less to say these days. It is all inside,' she taps her head with an arthritic finger, 'echoing through me in this house, the house of my family. I do not want to listen to the screaming of the past. I want silence. I am an old woman and I deserve some peace finally. I will live perhaps a few more years, or I will go suddenly in my sleep while I'm dreaming of that wide-open space where I see Ramón beckoning to me from a distance.'

A LIMITED ENGAGEMENT

Ronald Jenkins was in the habit of leaving his house on Calle López Peña at exactly one PM each day, Saturdays and Sundays excepted because Clara was home on weekends. He rose late, at approximately ten AM and had a breakfast of fruit, bread, and a nice piece of *queso* when it was available, with a cup of coffee. He usually finished his meal at about eleven AM then tackled a few chores. There was always shopping to do — that was his department since Clara was still working, as a teacher. Ronald had been in the military and when he'd retired with a good pension he'd begun travelling to Cuba, where he'd met Clara in the small town of Baracoa and soon moved in with her. There wasn't much available in the stores, so Ronald shopped on the black market, his purchases made around corners in darkened doorways. He managed to negotiate remarkably well considering he spoke hardly a word of Spanish, but he had mastered the bare essentials, after a fashion, and for the rest got by with a blustering kind of body language.

Today he'd risen later than usual and had decided to forego his shopping expedition because for once there was sufficient food in the refrigerator to hold them for a couple of days. He had lingered over breakfast and had even added a boiled egg to his usual repast, and then sat in his rocking chair on the front patio and read one of his mystery novels for exactly an hour. By twelve-fifty PM, with his face freshly shaven and splashed with cologne, he was ready to leave. As he passed Tarabel's house at the corner of Calle Ruber López he waved and stopped to exchange a few words with her little grandson, Quito, who was sprawled on his belly on the front step playing with a plastic Spiderman.

'*¿Ronaldo, porque tu no sabes hablar español?*' the three-year-old asked in response to Ronald's fumbled attempt at play.

'*Sí, sí, bueno!*' Ronald replied enthusiastically, having no idea that the boy was asking him why he didn't speak Spanish. Tarabel waved her plump brown arm and Ronald carried on, protected from the hot sun by a hat, sunshades, and a short-sleeved cotton shirt. It was the one Clara had given him for his birthday last year and he prized it greatly, even though she had shortly thereafter turned him out of the house, which at first had been a relief from their constant bickering and his almost total inability to understand her. He had returned to his own home in Western Canada where he'd soon fallen into the same trough of loneliness that had followed the collapse of his first marriage. When he could bear it no longer he returned to Baracoa on the pretext of attending the 500th anniversary of the foundation of the town, famous in Cuba as *La Ciudad Primada,* though the Baracoans always complained of being last when it came to receiving government perks. After a couple of weeks in a rental, Ronald had gingerly approached Clara in a gesture of penitence and she had opened her arms wide for him. Lately they had been getting along better, though her nightly excursions to the Pentecostal church were still a bone of contention, as were his afternoon excursions to Rumbo, his favourite bar, and to Parque Central in the evenings where he sat on a park bench with a mickey of home-brewed street rum in his pocket. He never got drunk. He was a disciplined man who limited himself to a certain number of drinks per day. Though that number was high, Ronald managed to maintain his equilibrium by pacing himself, keeping at it steadily, thus maintaining the conviction that he was drinking moderately.

He arrived at Rumbo at exactly one-fifteen PM and was just settling down at his usual table near the bar when Walter arrived. Walter was a bear of a man from the Maritimes, also retired from a career in the military, though in active service which Ronald had never seen — he'd been in accounting — so they had information to exchange on their differing experience. But, because Cuba has a way of pulling you into the moment, the major theme of their discourse was the scene playing out around them as they sat with their glasses of rum, and Ronald with his cigar balanced precariously on the edge of an ashtray. They watched the clientele come and go, commenting on the familiar faces of the locals mixed with new arrivals whenever a bus full of tourists arrived from Santiago. There were always some beautiful Cuban *chicas* for Walter to ogle, and occasionally they managed to persuade a couple of girls to sit with them. It was nothing to Ronald who was already married to a beautiful woman and whose only jealousy was of the Pentecostal church, but Walter was always on the lookout. Like Ronald, he spoke no Spanish, but he figured if his friend could catch a young Cuban wife, why not him too.

This was a special day — March 8th, International Women's Day. Walter was unaware of it, but Ronald had had it drummed into him by Clara that Women's Day was a big deal in Cuba, almost as big as Valentine's. He planned to buy a card for her at the kiosk outside Rumbo, and would pick a few flowers on the way home — he'd noticed a hedge full of red hibiscus behind the Catholic Church.

As he walked the short distance to the bar to order a second *trago* of Mulata, Clara was just beginning her lecture on Alejo Carpentier's Cuban classic *El reino de este mundo*. The members of Cubarumba were beginning their rehearsal for the evening's IWD performance, Tarabel was laughing with her husband Ulyses about Ronaldo's comical exchange with their grandson Quito, and Walter was eyeing the bounteous backside of a tightly packed Cubanita prancing up to the bar. When Ronald returned with his Mulata — a special treat on this day — Walter noticed that he was a little wobbly. And he saw a slight pulsing in the raised area over Ronald's heart, quite visible through the thin material of his shirt. 'How's the old ticker going, Ron?' he inquired.

'Can't complain.' Ronald patted his left breast. 'Did I tell you I'm planning to donate it to a Cuban?' It was a rhetorical question. He had mentioned it innumerable times.

As the adolescents settled to their writing exercise, Clara perused the pages of Carpentier's famous novel, her thoughts soon turning to her own library. It shone in her imagination like the Library of Alexandria, a massive enterprise stacked with all the wisdom and inspiration of the world's greatest writers. Ronald had recently presented her with a bookcase he'd had specially made by a craftsman carpenter who lived in the neighbourhood of El Paraíso where he went to buy his cheap homemade rum. They had placed the bookcase in the old garage out back, leaning it against the wall while the wood cured, and Clara had begun to plan the renovation of the garage and its transformation into a library. She would paint the concrete floor a deep red. She would look for a comfortable chair to sit in while she read, taking books down from her shelves one by one, sampling them, placing them aside on a small table which would match the chair. And of course, she would have a reading lamp — a free standing lamp — tall with an overhanging shade to cut the glare. Books were the stuff of Clara's dreams, principally of course the Bible, but always flanked and embellished by a world of literature — Martí, Shakespeare, Guillén, Ortiz, Loynaz, Barnet, Marquéz, Hemingway, Morejón, Villaverde . . .

She was startled out of her reverie by a voice from the open door. '*Clara, ¿podría venir a la oficina por favor?*' Could you come to the office please?'

Exactly five minutes after his second trip to the bar, Ronald doubled over in mid-sentence. His forehead hit the table causing it to tremble and topple his cigar, which rolled towards him, singeing his hair. He had been telling Walter about the time he'd fooled Cuban Customs, bringing in an electric toaster in his suitcase. He had been chuckling, his face reddened with merriment and then, as though something inside him had exploded, he was gone, drawn inside himself by something above and beyond his personal will.

They were immediately surrounded. Cubans are nothing if not vigilant. Who would have known that they were being so closely monitored? As though by magic Ronald was lifted and carried across the patio and down the steps to the open door of a car at the entrance to Rumbo. Walter stumbled behind him and crowded into the car with the others. In five minutes they were at the hospital, but Ronald was already gone, there was no reviving him. There were no heroic measures, no thumping of the chest as Walter had seen on hospital sitcoms — no isolation of the patient — just a cursory examination, right under his nose, in a side-room off the entrance to Emergency, and a matter-of-fact pronouncement of Ronald's death. The police arrived almost immediately, with a couple of stiff-faced immigration officials. The cops were young lads with stylishly shaven, perfectly shaped heads, but the officials seemed ageless. They'd never had a foreigner die in Baracoa, they said. There was no precedent for dealing with this. A careful procedure would have to be agreed upon.

Walter felt as though he was in a movie. The shock of it, the surprise! It couldn't be for real, there must be some mistake, it had all happened so fast, as though everyone in Baracoa had known that Ron's days were numbered and had been on alert for his collapse. The way they come out of the woodwork, Walter thought, like so many ants intent on carrying the body back to their den. All he wanted was to get out of that hospital room, and when Clara arrived he babbled the story to her unbelieving face and made his escape, refusing the bicitaxi boys outside the hospital, lumbering instead towards Parque Central like a lost buffalo. In the hurry he'd forgotten to pay his bar bill, and Ronald's — that was the least he could do. And he must knock back a final shot for poor old Ron.

It was determined by a couple of immigration officials that the cadaver must be removed to Santiago where it would await transfer to Havana for a post-mortem. 'This is the procedure which must follow the death of a foreigner on Cuban soil,' the stiffer of the two men explained to Clara. After searching through her house they found Ronald's health insurance certificate amongst his papers, and the wheels were put in motion for funds to be sent to cover the cost of transportation and post-mortem. The General Electric toaster, shining on the counter, was duly noted by the officials, with an almost imperceptible narrowing of their eyes — a Canadian brand unavailable in Cuba — but in the cause of compassion nothing was said. For the moment.

There was a brief gathering at the *funeraria* between six and seven-thirty PM, for Clara's friends and neighbours to pay their respects. Most were genuine, but there was a handful that came only because they suspected Clara would be receiving a widow's pension from Canada and thought it well to curry favour now in this important time. Tarabel came alone because Ulyses was too upset by the news. He was a sick man himself, about Ronald's age, and did not like to dwell on the topic of mortality. Several members of Clara's family came, including her brother Teo who was a drummer with Cubarumba. They would perform without him that night as he accompanied his sister on the road to Santiago de Cuba. At exactly seven-forty-five PM the funeral car departed, Clara hunched puffy-eyed in the front seat while Teo sat behind her with his firm hand on her shoulder.

It was well after midnight when they arrived on the outskirts of Santiago and began to cruise the streets, asking directions to the nearest hospital. They were sent first to the Provincial Hospital Saturnino Lora, named for one of the heroes of the War of Independence against the Spanish. After many wrong turns they arrived at Saturnino Lora and waited almost an hour before being shunted on to the Hospital Clínico Quirúrgico which dealt with international patients. After another long wait they were informed by the sleepy receptionist that the cadaver must first be registered with a Santiago funeral parlor. Having roused the night watchman of a nearby *funeraria* and filled out the necessary papers, they returned to Clínico Quirúrgico just as dawn was breaking. Clara was by now numb with exhaustion and readily agreed to have her husband's remains placed in cold storage while they waited for his insurance money to arrive by Global Excel so that they could proceed with his body to Havana — a journey of at least fifteen hours.

'Why can't the autopsy be performed here in Santiago?' Teo inquired.

The receptionist's heavily outlined eyelids widened very slightly in her stony face as her shoulders expressed the hint of a shrug.

Clara and her brother retreated to their aunt's house in the suburb of Abel Santa Maria, and there they waited for three days, by which time the insurance money had still not arrived, and Clara was persuaded to return to Baracoa in the safe embrace of her brother.

'It was Ronald's last wish to be buried in the cemetery in Baracoa,' she impressed upon the hospital officials before leaving Santiago. 'And he wanted to donate his heart to a Cuban,' she added.

'Too late for that,' Teo said.

'But his pacemaker,' she insisted, 'They must remove his pacemaker and donate it.'

Clara repeated Ronald's requests to the immigration officials in Baracoa. So long as they waited for the insurance money to come she felt his spirit hovering over her. She pictured him all around her, ephemeral as his cigar smoke, but just as persistent and aromatic. She smelled his after-shave cologne on their pillow when she buried her face in it each night and wept.

What with the distance between Baracoa, Santiago, and Havana, the difficulty with the telephones and the problems with computers, they lost track during the following weeks of the cadaver's whereabouts. With this news Clara's vision changed. She began to see her Ronald lying regally in cold storage, although she did not know exactly where, as he waited with dignity for his final resting place. He had always hated waiting — the endless queues for toilet paper, chicken legs, laundry soap, his favourite *queso* that arrived intermittently and mysteriously from Camagüey or Holguín, vegetables that came in from the countryside when there was sufficient fuel for *los camiónes*. Clara sat in her library and ran her hands over the smooth wood of her bookcase, recalling the perfection of her dream, and she wept to think that Ronald would never see the finished library, its shelves weighted down with literary masterpieces.

Walter had returned to Canada and once he was surrounded by everything familiar — his own language, his friends, his favourite foods — where could you ever find a good plate of fish-and-brewis in Baracoa? — even the doughy backsides of overweight women gave him more comfort than the magnificently formed orbs of those proud Cuban *chicas* — yes, when Walter found himself back in the bosom of his family the incident of Ron's death seemed like a dream. Though he couldn't banish it entirely from his mind, it did assume a comfortably fictional tone. Walter felt more than ever that he had been an extra in a Cuban film.

Ulyses regained his equilibrium and his skin took on a healthier tone as he began again to bounce Quito on his knee, and to laugh with his customary belly-shaking vigour at Tarabel's bawdy jokes. They saw Clara each day as she passed their door on her way to the high school and so they learned that she had been to the immigration office and had been informed by the secretary that the officials were working on her case but that there was no news as yet. One month to the day after Ronald's passing Clara took the initiative and phoned the Clinic in Santiago. She received the same message. They couldn't comment on the whereabouts of the cadaver at that time. The officials were working on her case. She would be informed when a decision had been made. Three weeks later, at the close of the school year, Clara travelled alone to Santiago. The cadaver was gone, they said, to Havana. It had left the previous week. When she phoned Hospital Cira García in Havana they knew nothing of it, nor did any on the exhaustive list of hospitals and clinics she phoned. Clara didn't have the money to travel to Havana and so she gave up her vigil. She sensed with the passage of time that her late husband had receded further and further from her until he had in fact returned to Canada where she had never been and now had no hope of going. This was not the case though, for Ronald's two sons knew nothing of his whereabouts. The

46

Jenkins boys travelled to Cuba to inquire, at first politely, and then angrily, as to the exact location of their dad's remains. How could a military man, always so precise and orderly, simply disappear? It was ridiculous!

'Of course,' said Clara with a patient smile, '*Pero no entienden cómo es en Cuba.*' You don't understand how it is in Cuba.'

Ronald's remains were never laid to rest in the cemetery high above Baracoa, where stone angels watch over the dead, their wings spread protectively, and where the sparkling ocean is visible in all her moods, evoked nightly by the dancers of Cubarumba as the Goddess Yemayá, the great mother who lives and rules over the seas in her swirling blue dress. Clara comforted herself with the thought that her Ronaldo was on a long adventure after his limited engagement with life. He had not liked travelling, preferring to move from A to B in the most efficient and familiar manner. He had always taken the bus from Havana to Baracoa rather than the plane because the bus was more predictable. Ronald had liked repetition. It had comforted him. He'd had no capacity for boredom. Perhaps, she mused, he has found in himself finally a sense of freedom and a love of travel. In her mind she created an epitaph for him that unwittingly captured the contradiction between his precarious existence and his desire for predictability.

Ronald murió como vivió, intensamente.

Ronald died as he lived, intensely.

∽∽∽∽

'Dad must be rolling in his grave,' Wayne whispers to his wife Sandy as yet another plate piled high with ham and cheese sandwiches is passed around. The house is unrecognizable from his previous visit when he and brother Pete had tried unsuccessfully to track down their father's remains. There are new floor tiles, new kitchen cupboards and counters, freshly painted bedrooms for Clara and her daughter Yuli, an extension on the back patio where the old garage used to be, a second bathroom, and now they're starting construction on the roof, to build a separate rental apartment. 'Well, good for her!' Sandy exclaims. 'Why not spend his money? The old skinflint!' It is Sandy's first trip to Cuba and she's quite taken with it all, especially with Clara and her Pentecostal friends, who are apparently responsible for the renovations. Wayne and Sandy haven't had a moment's peace since they arrived. The house is filled with workers who arrive at seven in the morning, and who hammer and saw all day, accompanying their noise with hymn singing. They are odd-looking people, Wayne thinks. He remembers his father's reluctance to become involved with the Pentecostals, always complaining about their presence in his house, though Dad's own friends are no prize — fat, beefy looking fellows of a certain age, all from Canada — and his Cuban friends, their number limited by Ronald's inability to speak Spanish, are alcoholics as he was. Rum perhaps has its own language, thinks Wayne, like the Pentecostal gift of tongues. There's a level of intoxication that carries one beyond language. He remembers falling victim to alcohol poisoning on his last visit and the strange altered state he had achieved, that had carried him through the nightmare of his dad's disappearance. 'Only in Cuba could this happen!' his brother Pete had ranted, while Wayne had maintained his cool throughout the misadventure. Now he has returned to Baracoa to celebrate his birthday with his stepmother and to help her with the bureaucratic rat's nest surrounding her Canadian widow's pension. Just as well Pete has stayed home in Calgary. 'You go,' he'd said, 'I've had it with Cuba!' After much finagling with both the Cuban and Canadian authorities they are down to the problem of Clara's name. She has four names, as is the Spanish style — Clara Isabela Montoya Velasquez — Montoya being her father's surname, Velasquez her mother's, and Clara Isabela her given names. Most Canadians have at most three names, reflected by the space allotted on the government forms. The length of Clara's name has become the sticking point in the approval of her widow's pension — there are not sufficient boxes for it — but Wayne is determined to find a way through. His philosophy is, "Barrel through with a smile till you get what you want." He's inherited his dad's steady dedication to routine but without Ronald's tendency to fluster and bluster, trying to cut economic corners. Wayne is determined to do right by his dad's widow.

'Where's the rum?' booms Walter, Ronald's Newfie friend who was with him at the moment of his fatal heart attack, and who has now returned to Baracoa for his annual visit.

'There is coconut water,' says Clara in her heavily accented English. She had known just enough English to hold her own in the endless squabbles with Ronald, usually about money and her desire for extensive home renovation. She has grown plump since his death, and is blooming, Wayne thinks, like a winter rose. She has a broad smile on her face, as does her daughter Yuli, also a devotee of the Pentecostal Church. They are obviously in their element with all these like-spirited folk in their home, transforming it according to Clara's long-held vision and nightly prayers. She received only a small amount of money immediately following Ronald's demise but, because of her faith in the rewards of prayer, she is going out on a limb with expensive renovations in the belief that the promised widow's pension will indeed come through. Wayne, the best chip off the old block of Ronald's essentially generous heart, layered though it was with miserly plaque and other constricting materials, is doing his best to see that she gets her due, especially now that she's pulling out all the stops for his birthday party.

Walter declines the coconut drink and instead plants a meaty hand upon his Cubanita's right breast. This is the only Cuban custom he follows, a gesture of ownership. Cuban women think nothing of it generally, but Walt's girl shifts uncomfortably in her seat, clearly embarrassed by the staring of the Pentecostal ladies in their sensible dresses and rubber sandals. La Cubanita wears strappy high-heeled platform shoes which accentuate the length of her shapely legs, and a skin-tight sheath of a dress which makes her feel naked in this particular setting. She grabs a sandwich as the plate passes by and gulps it down with a chaser of coconut water.

The band is just arriving, jostled by a constant stream of Pentecostal folk and neighbours dropping by to see what's on offer, leaving with plates of food to feed their entire families — sandwiches, *bocaditos* filled with ham paste, plastic cups of sweet coconut water with chunks of coconut meat floating in it, *ensalada fria* with cheese and pineapple, and tasty *croquetas*. Clara's brother Teo leads the band, setting the rhythm with his maracas, followed by two guitarists and a grinning percussionist who sits on his wooden box drum and coaxes a magical beat out of it. Cuban music is infectious, Wayne thinks, his usually unresponsive body beginning to pulse with the salsa rhythm. But the Pentecostals remain still as statues. Even though their church services include copious amounts of music and singing in which they join as one, they are not permitted to dance (and certainly not to drink), so the rhythm remains outside of them, keeping their souls free from the taint of it.

Wayne notices beads of sweat breaking out on Walter's brow. He won't be able to last much longer without a drink, Wayne thinks, and sure enough Walt stands suddenly, yanking his Cubanita to her feet. 'C'mon, let's go down to Rumbo and get a drink. ¡*Una cerveza!*' he articulates carefully, lifting his hand to his mouth like a bullhorn to make sure everyone understands. He slaps Wayne on the back, nods to Sandy and Clara, and heads out the door, his girlfriend tottering behind him on her platform heels.

'But the cake,' Clara calls after them, 'We haven't had the cake!'

A huge circular confection rests on her bedspread in the cool air of a whirring fan. It has been iced in an array of unnatural colours and is covered with blue sugar roses. Yuli and Clara carry in the cake between musical sets and present it to Wayne with a chorus of *¡Feliz Cumpleaños!* sung by the entire Pentecostal contingent and accompanied by the lead guitar. Teo sings 'happy birthday to you!' in his best English, learned during his one and only trip out of Cuba, when he toured Canada with his folkloric group Cubarumba. Though it is now thirteen years ago, the memory of that trip is as fresh in his mind as though he had returned only yesterday, because he relives it nightly as he lies beside his discontented wife waiting for sleep to come. He still has his treasured maple leaf sweater, a pair of worn-down runners, and a cracked mug from Niagara Falls.

Wayne receives the first piece of cake, complete with a swirling blue rose plunked atop the centre point of a big red W. The neighbours are already returning with empty sandwich plates held out for their share of cake. Clara beams, her new plumpness puffing her up like a prize chicken as she doles out mushy slices of cake beside the remains of macaroni salad. She is sharing her wealth finally, unfettered by Ronald's miserly ways. And if he did indeed roll over in his grave, what the hell! Wayne thought. He had loved his father but like all children had seen him clearly and somewhat critically, though it was his brother who had rebelled and argued with Dad while Wayne had been the peace-maker.

The cake is followed by pink ice cream cones, not exactly strawberry-flavoured, the fruit being suggested only by the pinkness of the frozen dairy product. The cones are cold and sweet, of no particular flavor, and they soon begin to drip onto the new flooring, making the tiles slippery and sticky. A strange elfin child appears, squeezing her way between the guitarists, and runs to her father who stands in the doorway. She looks like a stunted adult with a very old face, standing barely three feet high, brandishing her cone dangerously until her father takes it from her and holds the cone for her to lick. After a couple of slurps the child spots a woman across the room and lunges towards her, making odd keening sounds, unintelligible to Wayne and Sandy until they realize that the woman, who scoops up the little girl without a sound, is her mother — the likeness undeniable — and that she is deaf and speechless, as perhaps is her child, because when Yuli, who is a signer at the Pentecostal Church, begins to speak with her hands, the woman nods, her face suddenly animated as she signs back with one hand, holding the child balanced on her hip with the other.

Touched though he is by Clara's efforts on his behalf Wayne would like nothing better than to follow Walter to the bar.

'She's clearly doing it for her own benefit,' Sandy said, 'To impress her neighbours.'

'It's Cuban generosity,' Wayne protests.

'At your dad's expense?' Sandy retorts with raised eyebrows.

Wayne knows that Sandy is enjoying being fêted by the Cubans. It's just that this is her first visit and she has that edge of suspicion, not wanting to be taken for a sucker, which of course all tourists are. Wayne knows that the Cubans more or less starved after the collapse of the USSR, until the country opened up to tourism, and has lived off it ever since. He also knows that his dad had maintained a healthy sense of paranoia, which was the reason for his tight-fisted reaction to Clara's desires for home improvement. 'But Dad, just think what a good life we live here in Canada,' he'd said in a rare moment of disagreement, 'Anything you contribute to Cuba is a drop in the ocean of redress for an unjust and historically driven imbalance.' 'Don't try your fancy pants ideas on me, Bud,' Ronald had warned.

After the band's last song, *"Eternamente Yolanda"* — requested by Sandy who'd heard it in La Trova the previous night — after the last piece of cake has been carried across the street, after the *agua de coco* has been drained and all the dishes washed up by a team of Pentecostal ladies, Clara bids her guests farewell, her face still beaming and her cheeks flushed with success, then she kisses Wayne and wishes him a final Happy Birthday, and flops into bed beside Yuli who is already asleep. Only then does she drop her mask and shed a few tears for her Ronald who has left her so suddenly and unceremoniously. They are quiet tears for she is of necessity a practical woman, a thoughtful woman who cannot afford to wake her hard-working daughter who has to be up and out of the house early next morning. Clara had known from the beginning that she would be alone someday, for Ronald had been considerably older than her, and not a healthy man. But she had taken the risk. She had stepped out of her confined life and into a new life of adventure and possibility, though Ronald had kept her fettered for so long that she had quite lost face on her street. But that will change after tonight. She holds her newly plump cheeks in her hands and imagines they are Ronald's hands with that aroma of after-shave clinging, and just a hint of cigar smoke. She falls asleep like that, her cupped face resting on the damp pillow.

DANIELA'S CONDITION

On the afternoon of February 14th Daniela climbed five flights of stairs to the rooftop of her apartment building where lines of laundry were flapping in the wind. But that didn't concern her today — it was Saturday and she did her laundry on a Monday. Nevertheless, as she walked across the hot tarmac she couldn't help recognizing her neighbour's red dress, and the threadbare sheets and towels Kirenia was slowly washing to death.

Daniela had been at the school that afternoon, for the Valentine's Day presentation — *Día de los Enamorados* — a day second only to New Year's Eve when the entire nation celebrates the triumph of the Revolution. Iri and Eli had made special cards featuring big red hearts pierced by arrows. They had presented their cards, prompted by their teacher, after the children's singing was done. Daniela caught the look her husband had exchanged with Señorita Suárez. She knew that look. He's fucking her, she thought. The bastard. And Suárez wasn't the first one. How many times had he promised? *Nunca jamás, mi amor.* Never again, it meant nothing, you are my number one. Well, he had seven children with five different women, what kind of fool was she? Number one? No! Number five and still counting. Daniela had turned suddenly and left the celebration, telling Armando she had a headache. She was indeed giddy with the beer she'd drunk, but she had no headache. She simply couldn't bear to stay there a minute longer, watching him with her own children's teacher. The strange thing was that not a thought had passed through her head, no decision, no plan, she had simply turned and left as though some force from outside was guiding her. It felt good. She'd felt powerful.

Standing now on the rooftop, holding the cards with their pierced hearts, she sang quietly to herself, the love song that Iri and Eli had sung before the presentation. *Un corazón, otro corazón, a mi familia la quiero yo, un corazón, otro corazón* . . . She had worried so long about Iri's chronic shyness. Daniela had always been a shy girl herself so she understood how her daughter suffered, and she felt responsible for passing on that trait. She threw back her head and gazed into the sky. Ah, everything would soon change. Iri was on the verge of womanhood, and anyway, Eli had enough spark for both of them with her impish grin and adventurous spirit. She would look after her big sister. Daniela heard them in the distance, coming home along the narrow muddy path from the school — Armando singing in his husky voice, the girls chirping along with him. Eli shouted when she saw her mami, but Daniela just laughed and waved her arms. A couple of minutes later she heard their shoes clattering on the stairs, and then they were on the rooftop running towards her, Armando shouting, 'Daniela, *Ven acá*, come away from the edge! It's dangerous!' In that moment she took flight, without thought, her arms spread, her face turned to the blue sky as she plummeted. There was an instant of flurry as though wings were fluttering frantically to carry her, then a moment of blinding pain as something huge and invisible hit her full on and passed right through her body before she disappeared into an impenetrable darkness, as irresistible as the moment when they had placed the mask over her face for Iri's delivery.

In the days that followed there was talk in the neighbourhood of Armando's womanizing, of Daniela's timidity and bad housekeeping. Everyone felt sorry for the girls and fussed over them. Kirenia from next door, resplendent in her freshly washed red dress, greeted the children when they came home from school, and Armando's mother arrived to cook dinner each afternoon. Iri hid behind the solemn gaze of her brown eyes, but Eli, though her spirit was dampened, could still be enticed into a giggle, her wiry little body squirming with the unaccustomed attention. Kirenia took over the laundry while Aunt Laura cleaned the apartment top to bottom, clearing out the dirt and dust of years, grumbling all the while about Daniela's slovenly ways. Laura agreed to sleep over with the girls while Armando stayed at the hospital watching over his wife.

Daniela was a strong woman. Despite the shattering of her legs and pelvis and part of her spine she had survived, and she was not surprised to find herself alive for she had never planned her death. She had simply stepped off the edge in a moment of spontaneous freedom. When she opened her eyes for the first time and stared up at Armando from her hospital bed, she was confused to find herself encased in plaster from breast to toe. Only when she saw the cast did the pain of her shattered body begin to register.

Daniela's strange flight was the talk of Baracoa for weeks, stretching into months. At first the general opinion was that she had attempted suicide.

'How could she do that in front of her daughters?'

'God knows, she's suffered.'

'*Aiee chica*, but all men are the same. Whoring is no reason to jump off the roof.'

It seemed to some a cruel act of vengeance, coming as it did on Valentine's Day. 'A clear message if ever I heard one,' Armando's sister Laura said to their mother. The family sided with him. They had never warmed to Daniela, thinking her too silent and withdrawn — traits that they interpreted as her having an exaggerated opinion of herself — and she a mere *campesina!* She was his fifth wife, but their hearts were still with Mirian, the first wife and a woman of undeniable beauty and personality who was still very much part of the family. She lived beside the funeral parlour, round the corner from her ex-mother-in-law, and entertained a steady stream of lovers.

Armando insisted that his wife's fall had been an accident, that she had turned to him and the girls as they had burst onto the roof, and had somehow lost her balance and tumbled backwards. '*Gracias a Dios* her fall was broken by the branches of a *plátano*,' he said, 'She would have been dead for sure if she'd landed directly on the ground, especially with all that broken concrete in front of our building.' In those first days Armando had a strange light in his eyes, and he talked like a madman, repeating himself over and over, talking to anyone on the street who would listen. People thought he might wash his hands of it all when the shock wore off but, surprisingly, the accident brought out in him a gravity and compassion that no-one had ever guessed at. The miracle of Daniela's survival inspired in him a reverence that spurred him on in his efforts towards her recovery. To have been touched by death, to have survived that fall, his own wife! His energy surged as he rose early to make the girls' lunches and walk them to school, then he would go straight to the hospital to see Daniela and kiss her poor trembling hands, after which he would swing onto his bicycle and begin his daily tour of the town's schools where he was employed by the government as chief electrician. After work he would spend the evening at Daniela's side while family and neighbours took care of his daughters. Señorita Suárez received no more visits, no more secret messages or lustful glances from Armando as he checked the wiring of her classroom. It wasn't a matter of guilt, he just hadn't the time.

During her days in the hospital Daniela sought refuge in sleep, her body dragging her down to that dark place where the invisible force continued to collide with her, over and over, plowing through her body until she was hollowed out. Then the dreams stopped and she slept easily, breathing softly like a baby. Ten months passed before she was released, and by then Armando had learned from the nurses how to massage her feet and legs, how to insert a catheter, how to change her diaper, to handle her injections and pain medications, to bathe her and wash her hair as she lay prone on her bed. He set up for her a narrow cot under the window so that she could stare into the blueness of the sky and, when darkness fell suddenly as it does on the equator, bathe in the light of the stars, and of the moon as it reached its fullness.

On the day that Daniela arrived home and was carried on her stretcher up the four flights to their apartment, Armando felt transported, as though he were bringing home a bride, his sixth wife, an angel dropped from the heavens. Her passivity was thought normal at first but, as she emerged from her shroud of pain into an attention span long enough to watch a half hour episode of her favourite weekly *novela*, the family began to expect more of her.

'Leave her,' Armando said, '*No la molestes*. She almost died.'

His mother pursed her lips, but as time went on with no change in Daniela's condition the old lady spoke out, '*Mira!* She must do her part, Armandito. It's been more than a year. Tell her, she has to exercise her arms and legs and make an effort if she is to get better. How will she handle a wheel-chair with her arms all floppy from inactivity?' But Armando continued to defend his wife, and to minister to her needs which were constant and copious, and which became more demanding with the progress of her long recovery.

It was Kirenia who noticed the blossoming of Daniela. A woman dressed in red notices such things. '*Qué linda!* She's beautiful like never before!' Kirenia told the neighbours. 'Go see for yourself. She's plump and happy, her skin is shining, I tell you, she's a different woman, as though she was lit up from the inside.'

It was true. All that had been gathered within Daniela, suspended for a happier day, was now released. She had become a force like Mirian and all her other predecessors.

'What does he do now for sex?' Kirenia wondered aloud to the downstairs neighbour.

'*¡Dios mio!* Surely he's too tired to think of that with all this work on his hands?'

'But the way she looks at him,' Kirenia said, rolling her eyes suggestively.

The truth of it was that Daniela had found in her condition that which she had lacked — the ability to draw the full attention and devotion of her husband. She didn't mind when Laura and the mother came around nagging and criticizing, because Armando sprang to her defence, more devoted than ever. She no longer felt passive. She had learned to control him by her will, a force acquired in that moment of flight when she had let go of everything. How could she have guessed at such a twist of fate? And at how easily Iri and Eli would accustom themselves to Mami's new situation. They sat on Daniela's bed, Iri combing her hair while Eli chattered about her day at school, and when Armando came home she shooed the girls away and drew him to her with the power of her newly found will. '*¿Mi amor, como estas?*' he would ask. And she would raise her arms to cup his face, and pull him down to kiss her.

'I've ordered a wheelchair for you,' Armando said one Friday evening. 'It will be here next week.'

Daniela burst out laughing and threw her arms into the air. '*¡Vamos a bailar!*' she cried. 'You will dance me around the apartment in my new wheelchair!'

Armando began to laugh with her, though his was a husky broken sound, as he took hold of Daniela's hands and swayed her arms back and forth. Iri and Eli heard the laughter and came running into their parents' bedroom turning circles inside each other's arms, faster and faster until they were all spinning and laughing, and Eli began to sing — '*Un corazón, otro corazón*'... and Iri joined in — '*A mi familia la quiero yo.*'

It is April in Baracoa, the month when the winter gush of tourists slows to a trickle. Four years have passed since the accident, and Daniela's wheelchair rests in the corner of the bedroom a few feet behind her head where she cannot see it. The green plastic seat is covered with a thick layer of dust and grit which enters through the open window when the wind whips up, causing the *plátano* trees to sway and dance against a threatening sky.

Four more Valentine's Days have passed, and the girls are in a different school now. They are growing up and their father has aged beyond belief. His hair is grey and his back is stooped with the years of bending and lifting. Daniela on the other hand is flourishing, her skin smooth and plumped, her eyes sparkling, and on her moist lips always a radiant smile when he enters their room.

'*Mira, escuchame,* she must do her part, Armandito,' the mother says, like a broken CD, skipping and repeating endlessly.

'You must put her into an institution,' Laura says. 'She needs professional care.'

'In Baracoa? There is none,' Armando says wearily.

'In Guantánamo,' Laura insists.

He shakes his head sadly, 'I would miss her too much.'

'*¿Qué pasará con tu hermano?*' the old lady asks in a tremulous voice as she and Laura ride home in a bicitaxi. 'What if your brother has a heart attack with all this stress?'

'*Claro,* where will she be then? Who will look after her?' says Laura in her I-told-you-so tone.

Armando has tried and tried, but despite the fact that Daniela's arms have developed remarkable strength from hoisting herself up and wheeling herself about the apartment, her damaged spinal column screamed with pain at each jolt and turn, so that in the end she'd said, 'Take me back to bed, *mi amor*. I'm not ready for this chair. Put it in the *sala*. I don't want it in here reminding me.'

'There's no room in the *sala*. I have my bicycle there,' Armando had protested, and Daniela had smiled and shrugged, lifting her arms to him until he had leaned down and entered her strong embrace, lifting her slightly, pressed against him. Every time he touched her he felt that he was holding in his arms the miracle of life and death. He could not believe that she was still with him, the mother of his children, the woman who had flown through the sky to be with him. He was content to sleep alone in his bed, knowing that she was nearby, her brown face shining in the moonlight, her eyes open, vigilant, staring into the heavens.

The neighbours no longer talk about Daniela and her family. They have their own problems. Kirenia's red dress has become a cleaning rag with which she wipes the grease and grime from her broken two-ring burner. It is a mere scrap of cloth, so thin that she can hold it over her face like a skin graft and see every detail of her kitchen transformed by a rosy glow. She hasn't visited Daniela and the girls in more than a year. Let them fend for themselves. She has enough to do looking after her own family now that her husband has left, that bastard, running off to Santiago with the schoolteacher. How will she cook for her kids? The rice cooker is on the blink and now the burner has only one functioning ring. Perhaps she will ask Armando to take a look at it. After all he's an electrician. Neighbours must help one another.

Daniela lies in her narrow bed enjoying a sense of perfect balance. Armando takes care of everything. He washes her and lifts her and cleans her. He massages her legs every night and dabs perfume on her wounded thighs, in the crooks of her elbows, and at her wrists where the veins cluster. She does not think of the future. Illness is a country without past or future. It is a condition that has claimed Daniela as its own and that holds her in the eternal moment. She does not see the fading of her husband's definition, the paling and puckering of the skin around his eyes, the blurred dullness entering there. She has no fear for the future because it does not exist for her. She lies in her cot and gazes into that patch of blue sky glimpsed through the open window, where she has been hovering, a wingless bird, since *El Día de los Enamorados*.

BERTO'S KIDNEY

He had always enjoyed good health. Even as a child when his siblings and schoolmates were falling sick around him with *la gripe, la tos, dengue,* ear infections, Alberto had been a tough little lad. He spent his time on the street with a raggle-taggle gang, playing baseball with a makeshift bat and a small stone for a ball. He was a loose-limbed cheerful boy, but soon after his seventh birthday Alberto woke to a sense of neglect. Mamá had no time for him. Fredy and the twin sisters demanded all of Libya Castro's attention with their whining and snivelling. 'Go on with you, off to school,' she'd tell Berto as she hurried to the pharmacy to buy medicine for Fredy's cough, or antibiotics for the twins' *gripe.* It was a struggle with so little medicine available in Baracoa, always *el ultimo,* perched on the south-eastern tip of the island, far from the nation's capital which, even though it was situated at the *rear* end of the grand alligator which is Cuba, managed to gobble up all of the resources. Life in Alberto's household was a series of medical crises from which the healthy boy was excluded so he learned to take a back seat and help his mamá in small ways which she failed to notice, being in a chronic state of anxiety over the ill health of her children, and her own rising blood pressure, exacerbated by the philandering of a husband who rarely showed his face at home in the evenings.

But as the years passed Fredy and the girls grew out of their childhood illnesses and began to enjoy good health, a state which proved however to be temporary for once the twins were married, within a month of each other, and then Fredy too — moving in with the family of a plain though well-endowed girl one street over — they began to reproduce and were weighed down with the responsibilities of raising their own sick children. There were bills to pay, hungry mouths to feed, clothes to wash and, in the case of the sisters, infidelities to weep over at the kitchen table. As for Fredy, whose wife was faithful, though *insaciable en la cama,* his aches and pains increased with the years, his blood pressure rose alarmingly, and he had to take frequent time off work for emergency visits to the polyclinic which was unhappily located next door to the *funeraria.*

'Berto, help your brother!' Libya would snap. 'With all this time on your hands what else do you have to do?' For Alberto had not married, sadly. With the onset of adolescence he had retreated into the shadow of his good health and become an outsider in a town full of suffering neighbours. There was always someone laid out at the *funeraria;* sometimes two interments in one day making slow processions up the hill to the cemetery. The hospital was in a constant state of crisis with an overflow of patients and not enough beds — families had to bring fold up cots from home, as well as pots of *arroz con frijoles,* electric fans, radios, soap, drinking water. The polyclinic and the hospital were understaffed at the best of times, and with medical staff clamoring for missions abroad — to Venezuela,

Ecuador, Bolivia, Africa — the situation worsened. When an epidemic of *la gripe* hit Baracoa in the middle of winter with temperatures plummeting to twenty degrees centigrade and everyone shivering in long sleeved pullovers and jackets, the staff was unable to deal with the patient lineups of snorting, sneezing germ-carriers.

Alberto began to volunteer. He transported his neighbours for free in his bicitaxi, back and forth to the hospital, the clinic, the pharmacy — wherever they wanted to go — twenty times a day and into the night, following briskly trotting horses pulling wagons with oil lamps glowing in the darkness, slung low between the back wheels. Alberto felt sure that he would be contaminated by his close contact with the sick, but his robust health continued so he had nothing to contribute to the interminable organ recitals of his passengers. It seemed crass, and even cruel, to converse about his own good health, so he kept silent and contented himself at the end of the day with oiling and polishing his bicitaxi, sitting on the cracked leather of the recycled passenger seat, inhaling deeply, hoping to pick up a few germs.

There was no welcome for him in his mother's house. The very sight of her disgustingly healthy son disturbed Libya Castro and set her mouth in a line of discontent. Her only joy was the frequent visits of her sickly little grandchildren who were increasing in number. It seemed that ill health had not affected her daughters' fertility, and even Fredy had managed to father a couple of kids. 'I always thought *you'd* be the one to marry and get out of my sight,' Libya quipped. 'What ever happened to that pretty girl you were so stuck on in *escuela secondaria?* Too good for her, were you?' Alberto blushed like a boy at this mention of the girl with green eyes. She'd sat two rows over from him in grade ten, and they had smiled at each other every day, sneaking sidelong glances. He'd been full of hope and intention, and then she'd disappeared before he could ask her to be his *novia* — gone to Guantánamo, they said, with her family.

Alberto could bear it no longer — the painful memories, the loneliness, his solitary existence.

'Berto, *¿Qué pasa?*' asked Loli Legra, noticing the taxista's sad expression. Only last night Berto had carried Loli's wife to the clinic when her blood pressure had risen and frightened her, so he was feeling kindly disposed to his annoyingly healthy neighbor.

'Oh, my kidneys,' Berto cried, clutching at his waist, feeling for the appropriate place. He had a vague memory of anatomy from biology class in tenth grade. In reality he felt nothing, neither pain nor the usual pleasure of his well-being, for he had just entered a new zone where he was between fact and fiction. After three full days of complaint — which drew marvellous attention and even brought Mama Castro to his side, smoothing his brow and coaxing him with special foods — *un potaje de gandul, un postre de flan* made with the last of the eggs, floating in caramelized sugar — only on the fourth day as he once again furrowed his brow and contorted his mouth did he feel a real twinge of pain where he supposed his left kidney to be. He felt a mixture of alarm and gratitude. 'I am sick.' he whispered. 'I'm like everyone else. *Gracias a Diós!*'

Multiple tests ensued. Blood was taken, X Rays and ultra-sounds were authorized, pills were swallowed and more blood extracted until he felt quite genuinely weak. It was a marvellous feeling! But all the results were negative. Nothing could be detected and although Alberto was clearly not well he was sent home where he now had the undivided attention of Mamá, Fredy, his sisters, and the multiple nephews and nieces who gathered around Tío Berto staring solemnly, trying to prod his kidneys with their pudgy little fingers. Neighbours came to the door day and night with gifts of fruit, dishes of rice and root vegetables, medicinal teas brewed from the plants growing on their back patios — all the love and attention Berto had been missing. But love had come too late. His pretense had a firm hold on him and he was failing day by day. In the early hours of Sunday morning, with *regatón* blaring from Rafael's *fiesta de cumpleaños* up the street, Berto woke gasping for breath, and stared Death in the face as his left kidney tortured him with a screaming pain. At dawn he passed blood in his urine and was readmitted to the hospital, where he lay in the bed of an old woman who had died in the night. Berto panicked when he realized that Death had come to him only as a warning before moving on to the hospital to take the old lady in His skeletal arms.

But even though Death visited him each night on the hospital ward Berto was no longer afraid. In fact he began to look forward to the nightly visits as though greeting an old friend. 'Take me!' he begged. 'Take me please, I cannot bear this pain any longer.' The doctors thought he had a kidney stone and waited for it to pass because there was no space in the surgical schedule until the following week, but when Berto became hoarse with screaming they authorized an emergency operation. Berto felt himself drifting away under the anaesthetic and that was the last he knew until he opened his eyes to find Mami at his bedside holding his hand. Her eyes were full of concern as she told him that they had removed his kidney, a perfectly pink and healthy kidney with no sign of a stone in it.

'There's nothing wrong with this man,' growled the surgeon when he came on his rounds. 'He's a malingerer! Discharge him!' Alberto was taken home, hunched over in a bicitaxi, his loving mother at his side, which throbbed with the pain of his fresh incision.

'*Pobrecito,* my little Berto,' crooned Libya Castro. 'Does it hurt?'

'Yes, Mami, it hurts me terribly,' Berto replied.

'Don't worry, the stitches will come out in a week,' she said, patting his hand and kissing him with all the pent-up mother love withheld during his twenty-seven healthy years. What Berto failed to tell Libya was that the place where his kidney had been still tortured him. The pain of the incision and the tugging of the stitches were like a pleasant itch compared to the deep ache within his torso. Alberto was beginning to realize that the doctors didn't know everything, and he feared more than ever for his life, though there was a part of him that exulted in the situation. He had joined the cast and he was the star.

As Alberto lay in bed drifting in and out of consciousness he heard all the sounds of the street. He heard the cry of the vendors touting onions, tomatoes, malanga and boniato. He heard the *manisero* crying '¡*Mani, mani!*' and Eugenia in her *blusa roja,* (he had seen it often enough), calling '¡*Cucuruchu, cucurucho fresco!*' And all the while Libya hovered at his side, smoothing his brow, coaxing four-hourly doses of Ibuprofen down his throat with sips of water. He was afraid to drink too much now that he had only one kidney. He didn't want to overwork it. He wanted to live!

In the afternoon, after a brief nap, Alberto was roused by a rumbling in the distance. He felt more than heard it, his bed set atremble as the sound came closer. *¡Basura, basura, saca tu basura!'* Ah, it was the garbage men calling. He smiled to himself, his eyes still closed as he savoured the familiar sounds. He heard footsteps coming and going — his father carrying buckets of water from the cistern to the kitchen, he supposed, and his mamá bustling about the house, but when he opened his eyes a strange figure was standing over him; not his mamá, no, nor his sister nor any of his neighbours. The girl bent down until her green eyes were on a level with his. 'Don't you remember me?' she asked. 'I'm Gloria — Gloria Amor from tenth grade.' Alberto came to with a jolt and held his breath, waiting for the pain of his ghostly kidney to kick in. 'I have returned to Baracoa now, graduated as a doctor. Where does it hurt, Berto?'

He took her hand, which was delicate and fragrant with fine blue veins just visible under creamy skin, and he placed the wonder of it over his own heart. Of course he remembered Gloria Amor with her thickly lashed green eyes, luminous as the River Toa in summer when it shimmers under the sun's intense heat. *'No te he olvidado por un minuto,'* he said, 'But I never expected to see you again.'

Gloria came each day and sat with him. She told him about her life in Guantánamo where she had pined for Baracoa and decided that when she graduated she would return to work there. She told him about her new job at the polyclinic. She impressed him with her passion to heal the entire ailing population of Baracoa, and Berto found himself unlocked, sharing with Gloria all the secrets of his solitary life. After a few days, when he was strong enough to sit up in bed, he asked her, 'Would you have come to me if I hadn't been sick, Gloria?'

'¿*Cómo no*, Berto?' she replied with a smile. 'It was always my intention to come and find you, but you made it easy for me. When we are all together in our illness, it is easier for us to find each other and move forward with the power and force of our collectivity. Blessed are the weak for they will inherit the earth; Matthew, Chapter 5, verse 5.' She leaned into him, touching his hand gently as her lips parted, revealing small glistening teeth, and just the very tip of her pink tongue. It was only later, much later, when Gloria and Berto were married with twin boys, and had become devoted members of the Pentecostal church — which Berto had learned from Gloria was yet one more way to join in the collectivity of his people — that he realized her misquotation, or perhaps his own misunderstanding of it,' but by then it did not matter. He had regained his strength and with it had found true meekness.

◦◦◦◦

W hen Evangelia came home it felt like the end of the war. People stood in darkness waiting for the cars to come, with only faint lights from their houses spilling onto the street. Horatio's jeep came first, his family crowded in and Horatio himself barely visible amidst the bags and parcels filled with goods from Venezuela.

Venusa wrung her hands nervously as though she were washing them, awaiting her sister's first homecoming leave with a mixture of longing and trepidation. She'd fought with Evangelia before her departure a year ago and had repented ever since. 'You can't go!' she'd said, 'It's too dangerous in Venezuela! Please, Evangelia, we can manage without the extra money.' And Evangelia had replied with uncharacteristic passion, 'I know you're jealous, Venusa, but don't try to stop me! It's my only chance! I'm fifty-one years old! This is a gift from God. Tomás was in Angola for two years, Felix was in Leipzig, two of the other nurses at the clinic have been on missions — why not me? It's my turn!'

Evangelia's grand-daughter Milena skipped through the house, her little sister Eleana stumbling behind her on bowed legs, trying to keep up as Milena raced onto the front patio and darted across the street, dodging traffic. 'Milena! *Ten cuidado!*' Venusa yelled.

Yarisnelda arrived next in a big old Chevrolet rolling down Calle Mariana Grajales, and everyone cheered as though she were the queen, except Venusa who had a sudden feeling of panic, as though something dreadful might happen — an accident in the darkness perhaps, where the sewer pipes were being laid. She let out a little cry then clamped her hand over her mouth, and pointed up the street. There was Tomás following behind the Chevrolet in a borrowed car, driving with a slow dignity which seemed ceremonial but was more likely due to his unfamiliarity with driving. In Angola he'd driven army vehicles, but in the two decades since coming home he'd been lucky to find a functioning bicycle to ride to work.

Venusa glimpsed Evangelia as the car door opened, and in the same moment a couple of dozen neighbours sighted her and a cry went up like the roaring of an animal. Venusa was surprised by sudden tears as a shameful emotion rose in her, like a response to the playing of the national anthem on television when Fidel spoke from the Plaza de la Revolución. Venusa's eyes searched frantically for the children as she screamed, 'Milena! Eleana! *Ven aquí.*' Evangelia stepped out of the car and everyone surged forward, hiding her from view with a multitude of hands and arms and bobbing heads. Tomás climbed out on the driver's side, his face impassive. Three of the sisters from the Pentecostal church spilled from the back of the car with Morito, Evangelia's son-in-law, gathering parcels and bags in their arms, everyone strangely solemn, intent on their task. They'd all been waiting so long. Milena and Eleana appeared out of nowhere, jumping up and down, screaming 'Abuela! Abuela!' and Evangelia scooped them up just as Big Marta from the church enveloped her in a strong-armed embrace.

The crowd began to part but Venusa hung back. She felt shy and out of place. Evangelia looked different, her hair a mass of golden-beaded braid extensions, her face calm and beautiful as ever. She wore skin-tight jeans and an indigo-gold blouse that revealed the generous swell of her breasts. On her sturdy feet she wore golden jewelled sandals, and there were large gold pendants dangling from her ears. This is a new Evangelia, Venusa thought. She's coming home like a victorious warrior bearing the spoils of sacrifice. And it isn't only the clothes. There's something else. She has a new way of carrying herself. Venusa crossed her arms over her scrawny breast and pressed herself against the wall of the front room. I should go back to the kitchen, she thought, make myself useful. But neighbours were crowding into the house looking for the *Bienvenida* cake and refreshments and Venusa couldn't move. Then she saw her opportunity, slid between Big Marta and her daughter Dulce, and shyly approached Evangelia who embraced her with such warmth that soon the two women were crying on each other's shoulders. Nothing was mentioned of their parting disagreement. It was as though they were children again, always together, the first two in a family of fourteen. They couldn't afford to be at odds. They broke their embrace and held each other at arms' length, then Evangelia linked arms with Venusa and laid her head on her shoulder as they walked together down the corridor to the kitchen.

The cake was already gone, leaving the children smeared with greasy pink icing, and the floor sticky with spilled orange crush and kola. Men were gathered in the yard at the back of the house, handing rum bottles around. But not Tomás. He had quit before Evangelia left for Venezuela — he'd had to — he was killing himself with weekend binge drinking. He'd been on medical leave for nine months and had only recently returned to work, not in the slaughterhouse, but a lighter job in the crafts centre where he prepared big chunks of pungent guayacán for carving. Artisans transformed the wood into curvaceous dancing girls and spear-handling Taíno warriors. Tomás showed little emotion about his wife's return, but everyone knew that he'd been waiting for that day, checking his cell phone for messages from her, fretting when the money ran out and he had no way to recharge it. His welcome was clear in the condition of the house — it was sparkling clean, and he'd fixed the window shutter that had been dangling for years, put a new battery in the wall clock, scrubbed out the bathroom, and even made a tiny room for Milena by blocking off part of the kitchen. She was turning into a *señorita,* unwilling to go on sharing a bedroom with her parents and little sister, or with her grandparents. In Baracoa everyone lived together — there was no alternative — but with the extra money Evangelia received for her work in Venezuela they'd be able to start construction on the roof when building materials became available, and soon a couple of new rooms would sprout there with a view of the jungle strip that ran between Mariana Grajales and El Castillo — the hotel that towered above the town of Baracoa. Tomás remembered Tío César telling him about the old days when Batista's men had imprisoned the revolutionaries in El Castillo, and tortured them in what was now the Dining Room. With the triumph of the Revolution in '59 the soldiers were driven out, 'Flung from the crocodile's snout north to the tail of La Habana and Raúl's firing squads,' Tío had said with a flourish of his muscled arm. César had been a revolutionary himself — an electrician and explosions expert.

Bags were unzipped, suitcases snapped open, gifts spilling out. Eleana's little feet lit up with the red flashing lights on her new Venezuelan shoes as she pranced around the front room pushing a doll's carriage. The naked doll sat rigid, one arm dangling precariously while Eleana pulled the cord in back of its neck over and over, playing a reggae tune, faint below the din of the neighbours' celebrations in Horatio's and Yarisnelda's houses further down the street. Milena burst from behind her curtained room in a pair of *calenticos* — very short shorts that revealed every crack and curve of her emerging form. *'¡Peligroso!'* exclaimed her step-father Morito, slapping her bottom. Just then the girls' mother, Ariadne, arrived home from work and pushed her way through to embrace Evangelia. Mother and daughter clung to each other for minutes as Ariadne wept all her bottled-up tears. When she disengaged herself finally, snorting and wiping her wet face with her arm, she smirked at Morito and shouted — 'What the hell you looking at?' She disappeared into the bedroom with Evangelia and when they emerged a few minutes later Ariadne was transformed in skin-tight white jeans, a plunging turquoise blouse, hooped white earrings, and a tottering pair of white sandals.

When the rum bottles were empty the crowd began to thin. Venusa gathered all the gifts and wrapping paper strewn about the house and piled everything on the tattered old sofa in the front parlour. There had been no gift for her, but Evangelia's homecoming was gift enough.

Evangelia yawned and sighed, almost asleep on her feet. After all, she'd been travelling since six that morning when the group left Caracas by plane for Santiago de Cuba, then a long wait for the bus to Guantánamo, more than five hours on the road, finally curving along La Farola highway to Baracoa.

'Come, my sister, you must sleep,' Venusa said, leading her down the corridor.

Tomás was waiting at their bedroom door, leaning against the doorjamb, his dark eyes watching Evangelia. But she lingered with her big sister, laughing about Venusa's drunken husband, José. 'You'd better leave him in my backyard for the night,' she said. 'Let him sleep it off.' She knew the scene too well. But now her reformed husband awaited her and she turned to him with a tired smile.

When Venusa passed by on her way home from work a couple of days later Evangelia was on the front patio. The sisters embraced and moved through the house to the kitchen where it was more private. Venusa noticed that Evangelia had regained her habitual slouch, despite the new clothes and shoes.

'I'm not feeling so good, Venusa. I have pains in my stomach,' she said. 'No, no!' she held up her hand as Venusa opened her mouth to speak. 'I don't want to go to the polyclinic.'

'Why are you so stubborn? You won't let me help you.'

'Venusa, *no entiendes. Mira,* I have twenty-five years' experience as a midwife and what do they do? They send me to Venezuela to teach the nurses there how to do safe deliveries.'

'What does that have to do with your stomach pain?' Venusa asked.

'All the experienced doctors and nurses are away on missions,' Evangelia explained. 'Cuba has a reputation outside, but her own people have to suffer with newly graduated medical staff who lack experience and have to work without guidance. Now do you understand why I don't want to go to the polyclinic? Those kids know far less than I do!'

Venusa nodded her head back and forth, weighing this information. 'Maybe you're right,' she said. 'My goddaughter was sent home from the hospital with her five-year-old the doctor said he had *la gripe*, two days later the boy died from pneumonia.'

'Ah,' Evangelia nodded knowingly. 'Yarisnelda's grandson died while we were in Venezuela. Undiagnosed bronchitis.'

'And my neighbour's daughter, Floriana, she died from an anaesthetic,' Venusa said, her eyes widening as she began to put the information together. 'It was a routine operation to remove an enlarged mole. Such a tragedy. She worked in the bank. She was young.'

The sisters looked at each other and shrugged.

'*La vida*,' Venusa said.

'*Como Diós quiere*,' Evangelia replied.

A week passed before their next chance to talk, and by then the upper part of Mariana Grajales, where it crossed Calle Calixto García, was in total disrepair. It looked like a war zone with the innards of the street laid bare by huge serrated-digger machines. The new pipes, five feet or more in diameter, lay on the red excavated earth, waiting to be dropped into place by the massive jaws of a hydraulic arm. There was a plank laid across the abyss, serving as a bridge for people to maneuver on foot or with bicycles, crossing with held breath before speeding down the hill, avoiding deep potholes. Venusa had crossed safely and walked down the hill to find Evangelia on the patio as usual, dressed in her old *bata de casa* — a shapeless dress that shrouded her magnificent form and looked rather strange with her golden-beaded hair extensions. Like her daughter Ariadne, she had a sulky expression, but Venusa knew her too well to be fooled by that. A kiss, a caress of her cheek, a teasing word, and their old rapport was re-established as Evangelia's head inclined and a smile tugged the corners of her mouth. *'Mi hermana,'* she said tenderly, 'Where have you been?' They sat in the *sala* and Venusa asked finally, the question that had been on the tip of her tongue since the homecoming, 'How is life in Venezuela?' 'It's very dangerous,' Evangelia said, 'They'll kill you for a pair of shoes.'

'But what about Chavez? Doesn't he help the people?'

'He does so much for the poor, and he's popular, but there are those who hate him and spread propaganda. There's an election coming, Venusa. I know he'll win, his fourth term.'

'But they said on the news he's in La Habana again, having more treatment for cancer,' Venusa said. She worried that if Chavez' health failed they could enter another "Special Period," as Fidel had called it when the USSR fell and Cuba had been starved for five years. Those who remembered said that the Special Period never ended, only that the survivors got used to it, that deprivation became normal. And the younger generation knew no different. Their parents sacrificed for them when they were little, but as adults they sought their own survival through foreign lovers. Look at Rosa Carceles, Venusa thought, with her *extranjero* who came from París three times a year with expensive gifts, and promises of a French passport.

'We can't go out after six o'clock in the evening,' Evangelia said. 'You were right, Venusa. It's a dangerous country. The Catholic priest was murdered, and our pastor received death threats.' Evangelia was a fervent Pentecostal. In Baracoa she attended services three evenings a week, and she believed it was her prayers that had brought about Tomás' reformation. 'We can't meet, we can't pray, we can't sing.'

'What do you do?'

'I live with a surgical nurse from Havana and a midwife from Guantánamo. We have a computer. I write to Tomás. That's how we spend the evenings.'

Venusa nodded, her eyes blank. What did she know about computers? She saw the kids in the park with their phones, that was all. People used to talk to each other face to face.

'I don't want to go back, Venusa. But I have to, at least for another year. Tomás has applied for a permit to build — two rooms on the roof, for Ariadne, Morito and the girls, with their own kitchen and bathroom.'

Eleana was watching a video, still kicking her feet with the red lights blinking on the toes and heels of her new shoes. The child leaned forward to turn the sound up higher, sucking her thumb and wiggling her little butt to the reggae beat.

'I have to do the laundry, but there's no water,' Evangelia sighed. 'They told us it would be off for three days, but it's already been five days and now there are problems.'

Venusa shook her head. Five days could turn into fifteen with the condition of the roadworks. No wonder my sister is tired, she thought, coming home to this. I remember how she longed to get out of Cuba and see the world, but it's been a disappointment.

The next time she saw Evangelia was in the centre of town the following week, with Tomás and Ariadne. Evangelia waved a sheaf of papers at her. 'We have the permit,' she said with just a touch of enthusiasm.

'*¡Qué bueno!*' Venusa exclaimed. '*¡Felicidades!*'

'Now we have to wait for the materials,' Ariadne said sulkily.

'How long?' Venusa asked.

Tomás looked down at his shoe and scuffed it on the sidewalk; Evangelia greeted a passerby; Ariadne shrugged and sighed in a long slow expression of resignation. Venusa understood. She too had been disappointed many times and had learned to be discrete. It might be a matter of months or even years before the building materials could be purchased — depending on availability. And need. If another hurricane hit later in the year, building materials would go first to the affected areas.

'When are you coming to my house?' Evangelia asked with a sudden sense of urgency.

'When are you leaving?'

'Tomorrow. Or the next day. I'm waiting for news.'

'I'll come tonight.'

Several dates were set and then changed. All the returnees were in suspense, waiting with their empty suitcases, but it was to be a full week before everything was firmed up, and even then, who was to know after so many delays that there would not be yet another. 'You must come to the terminal,' Evangelia said emphatically. 'I'll be waiting for you on Sunday at five in the afternoon.' She was to take the bus to Guantánamo, and on to Santiago de Cuba, then a plane to Caracas, retracing her steps.

Venusa arrived at the bus terminal at five thirty, half expecting them not to be there — another change and no way of letting her know — but yes, there they were, Evangelia and Tomás lounging under the ceiba tree with its sprawling branches trailing to the ground. All the travellers were there with their families ready to see them off. Horatio and Yarisnelda both said the time had gone too fast, and Yarisnelda was red-eyed, still grieving for the grandson who had died so suddenly in her absence. Horatio's son clung to his papa, while his mami held onto the baby. She'd been pregnant when Horatio left a year ago and now the child, already ten months old, had met her papa for the first time. They sat around talking and joking as though it were just another day.

'Do you have your ticket?' Venusa asked.

'Morito will take care of it,' Evangelia said with a shrug.

People milled about, unconcerned. Some walked into the terminal building to see what was happening, and finally Horatio returned with the news that the bus from Guantánamo was delayed. There had been a breakdown, he said, and they were making repairs. By seven o'clock everyone was hungry and thirsty, but the terminal cafeteria was closed, though even at the best of times it served nothing more than beer and pop, and occasionally *cucuruchu*, a sweet mash of cacao, coconut, papaya, orange rind and honey spooned into a palm leaf cone. The energy of the waiting group was beginning to droop like the ceiba branches when, with a sudden flurry of dust, the bus rumbled down the Malecón and through the terminal gates. People began to embrace and make their farewells, though no-one yet had tickets. They didn't go on sale until the passengers from Guantánamo were disembarked. 'No problem,' said Evangelia, 'We *misioneros* have priority.'

Venusa was beginning to feel very sad at the thought of parting with her sister again. She was anxious about the last-minute rush for tickets, the uncertainty of it all. Evangelia was making her slow way into the terminal, moving from one embrace to another. Big Marta was there to bid farewell and to give God's personal blessing to the mission. Milena was on the verge of tears so that Venusa couldn't get a word out of her, but Eleana was too young to understand that her *abuela* was going away again, and she babbled away, singing and hopping like a little bird in her blinking shoes.

Morito stood tall amidst the crowd, trying to get the attention of the ticket vendor, then he was swept suddenly towards the door with a wave of passengers bursting through, brandishing their tickets for inspection. Milena had begun to cry noisily, huge tears rolling down her cheeks as she clung to her *abuela*. More of the *compañeras* from the church had arrived and surrounded Evangelia, praying and blessing her amidst their tears. Ariadne pushed them aside and embraced her mother, sobbing with a passion equal to that of her own Milena; and Eleana began to howl, her little hands grabbing at her mother's plump thighs. Evangelia has become a *personaje* once again, Venusa muttered to herself, a celebrity amidst her own family, on the verge of her departure. And she too began to weep, caught up in the emotion of the crowd. Evangelia alone remained calm.

Venusa wiped her eyes and looked around for Tomás. Through the murky glass of the waiting room she could see the bus filling with passengers, the driver already in his seat, the ticket collector waving his arms and shouting emphatically at Morito while Tomás stood quietly off to one side. It was at this moment that Evangelia appeared, ready to board finally, with Ariadne behind her carrying her bags. But somehow Evangelia's ticket had not been reserved, and the ticket collector said there was no room for her on the bus. A discussion followed about standing room, at least until Guántanamo, but the driver shook his finger. '*Absolutamente prohibido. Demasiado peligroso.*'

And so Venusa watched with mixed feelings as the bus lumbered through the terminal gates and disappeared in a cloud of black exhaust. Perhaps my sister can stay home now, she thought, but she knew that in reality Evangelia had to complete her mission. An unaccustomed wave of anger and frustration swept over her. If only Evangelia had been ready, lined up with the other passengers, prepared and insistent. But no-one except Venusa seemed concerned. Opinions were exchanged, accompanied by lackadaisical gestures while Evangelia simply shrugged in her seductively boneless manner. Tomás took hold of her arm and they spoke briefly with her young brother Felix, who had appeared out of the darkness with a bicycle and now pedalled away with Morito balanced precariously on the crossbar.

'How will you get to the airport?' Venusa asked. If only her sister could have taken one of the twice-weekly flights to Santiago, but they wouldn't pay for that, and in any case the flights were filled with tourists.

'Morito will find a car,' Evangelia said calmly. 'We're going back to the house. Come with us.'

And so she went, arms linked with her sister, who was linked in turn with Tómas, while Ariadne went ahead with the children on her bicycle — Milena balanced in front of her and Eleana straddling the rat-trap with her chubby arms clasped around Ariadne's broad hips. The worst part was the anti-climax after all those tears and heartfelt goodbyes, but it prolonged Evangelia's status for a few more hours, it singled her out, the only *misionera* left behind.

It was past midnight when Morito and Felix arrived in an old Toyota Cressida driven by a friend of Morito who agreed to drive them overnight to Santiago de Cuba in time for Evangelia to board her plane to Caracas in the morning. How will they pay for it? Venusa wondered, but it seemed to have been worked out by the men, so she decided to stop worrying. She kissed Evangelia one last time and, exhausted with all the goodbyes, walked slowly homewards through the warm night, smiling to think of Tomás and Evangelia in the back of their car, asleep in each other's arms. She tried not to feel envious, knowing though that she would probably find José already snoring with an empty rum bottle beside him on the crumpled sheet.

The street was so badly lit that she almost tripped when her toe caught the rim of a pothole. It was a new one, the concrete sidewalk beginning to wear away outside Big Marta's house. Venusa could hear them singing inside, a hymn of glory to speed Evangelia on her way. She hesitated, almost ready to join them, to give herself the comfort of singing with her *compañeros*, but something tugged at her, she needed to go home. As she approached her own house, walking more carefully now, she saw someone on the front patio. Was it her son? Or perhaps her brother Felix. She squinted in the gloomy light but she couldn't recognize him — a man for sure, but who? She walked faster now, and as she reached her house she grasped the handrail that skirted her patio. Venusa peered across the railing, then she shook her head and laughed. It was José, looking at her with a steady gaze, his dark eyes full of expression, as though he had been waiting for her. *'¿Qué pasa?'* she asked. Did something happen? But he didn't answer. He shrugged almost imperceptibly and reached for her, so Venusa put her hand in his rough, worn hand, and with his touch everything became vivid, every detail of his tired face sharp and clear after her confusion in the darkness. How could I not have recognized my own husband? she wondered, with a guilty pleasure. She saw in the half-light how José's grizzled hair stood out like a halo around his head, and how his shirt clung to his wiry frame. She could count every rib on his chest. Venusa would have been content to simply enjoy that moment, but José pulled her down onto his lap and set them both in motion, rocking together in the *balánce* as he wrapped his strong arms around her and nuzzled her neck. He smelled pleasantly of sweet tobacco, not a drop of rum on his breath.

෴

THE PIANO-TUNER
FROM GUANTÁNAMO

Mári has been waiting all morning. She's dusted the piano three times and arranged the bench exactly so — any number of times — now she sits in her rocking chair, waiting. He will arrive on the noon bus with his son to guide him, and the driver will put them down at Calle Moncada, as arranged, and they will walk up the hill to her house.

The old upright stands waiting on the far side of the *sala*, its keys a mottled brown like tobacco-stained teeth, but Mári has dusted the vase of roses that sit atop the instrument. It had belonged to her father who played exclusively the music of worship, and upon his death it had passed to her brother Reymundo who had played every kind of joy, from Sunday hymns to jazz and salsa. On Fridays they'd held Danzón evenings, which had brought elegant old couples drifting into the *sala* where they would dance sedately to the romantic beat, the ladies sporting gorgeous fans in their right hands while the men, full-handed, guided them effortlessly across the polished floor. Even as a girl Mári's heart had swelled with the music and the dignity of the ladies as they danced. Now she is herself a lady *en la tercer edad* — the final stage of her life — living with her daughter Gabriela, and the two grand-children — Alegra, who is studying to become a doctor, and her athletic grandson, Yorki, who has his heart set on a career in sports and has already won three medals for sprinting. Mári is immensely proud of the boy.

When she hears a gentle tapping she immediately opens the door and blesses her visitors with a smile. Her spirit illuminates the house, making of it a beacon at the corner of Moncada and Rodney Coutín, and when she makes her weekly pilgrimage to the church across town, her arm linked comfortably through Alegra's, she greets her neighbours with a Biblical salutation and that same radiant smile, as though she were spreading her wings across the town of Baracoa. Mári's grace and ageless beauty draw people to her and incline them to listen to her Baptist discourse without resentment.

Osvaldo helps his father over the threshold. Despite a boyish appearance Osvaldo is thirty-five years old and has already been accompanying Oriol for more than twenty years. The old man flexes his fingers and inhales the humid air of Mári's front room, his body swaying from side to side, his eyelids flickering. With Osvaldo's guidance, he feels his way from chairback to wall until, together, father and son locate the piano on the far wall of the *sala* where the light comes from behind, illuminating the chipped ivories.

'Nobody plays now except my cousin Melva,' Mári says, 'But I have plans.'

She recalls last year's Baptist convention when Melvita, who shared the old family home in Santiago with cousin Gertrudis, had travelled all alone to Baracoa, because Gertrudis had to give her testimony yet again. How straight-backed had been

Melvita's comportment as she'd sat at the piano plunking out her hymns while Mári stood beside her, puffed like a songbird, rendering love songs to the Lord in her vibrato soprano. Alegra had tinkered for a while, but she was working at the hospital all day and in the evenings she had to study for exams, so the piano has been largely neglected while Mári has scrimped to gather sufficient funds to pay the piano-tuner's bus fare and accommodation for a night at her friend Erminda's *casa particular* down the street.

Oriol refuses Mári's offer of coffee, but his son drinks a small cup of the dark sweet liquid to fortify himself after the journey — three hours, much of it on La Farola, a winding road carved out of the dense jungle that hides Baracoa from the eyes of the world. Until the construction of the highway the town had been accessible only by the ocean which has lapped its shores since the beginning of time, worrying away the land in grains of sand, then sucking it up and throwing it back onshore.

Mári returns to the kitchen with the empty cup, not wanting to disturb the men while they work, but when strange sounds reach her ears she hovers in the central courtyard of the house, peeping around the corner to watch. She sees the piano laid bare like a patient undergoing surgery, and the tuner sitting erect, chin tilted with an air of absolute concentration as his fingers rest on the keyboard, pecking persistently at each note while his son adjusts the strings. Mári can barely hear the old man's voice. All the energy is in his listening, followed by the intimacy of a few whispered words. Osvaldo follows his father's instructions silently, tightening with *un martillo de afinación* held between thumb and forefinger, pinging with *el diapasón* to fine-tune the strings.

After a while Mári tip-toes to the back of the house and sits on her bed to read the Bible, but there is a persistent ringing in her ears, a presaging of something wonderful as she imagines the lively sounds that might emerge from the old piano, as though they had been crouching there inside awaiting their chance, just as in the days of Reymundo's spontaneous concerts when he would sit with a glass of rum in his left hand — though when their mother was in the house he would hide that glass in the corner between piano and wall. Reymundo drew such sweet inspiration from the fiery alcohol that Mári wondered if it really was a sin to drink, as her Baptist minister preached. She had loved her brother fiercely until the end, even though he had caused his family great suffering with his drinking and womanizing. He had been a *mujeriego* of the first order! It was his infidelity that had pained Reymundo's wife — even more than the violence that had left her children timid and silent.

Mári has just reached the verse where Job declares to God, 'My ears had heard of you, but now my eyes have seen you,' when she hears the cascading notes of a classical masterpiece! It is the tuner who plays and he is a wonder to hear with his fingers flying across the freshly tuned keys, reminding her of the waterfall she saw on a school trip to Parque Alejandro Humboldt so many years ago, but that she has never forgotten.

Osvaldo stands by patiently, and when the Schubert Impromptu is done he says, 'We must move on now, Papi, to Casa Yánis.'

'You must cross Moncada,' says Marí, 'and walk two blocks towards Parque Central. Yánis lives in the blue house on the right, beside *la panadería*.' She delves into the pocket of her apron where a fold of crumpled notes nestle, and hands them to Osvaldo who pockets the bills without counting them. The money has passed through too many anxious hands and has the sour grey smell of accumulation. Oriol, his left arm resting on his son's shoulder, offers his own cool hand to Mári who clasps it and thanks him, bestowing the Lord's blessing upon him as he departs from her house.

Mári closes the door, walks over to the piano, and reaches with her hand to touch the keys. As she presses middle C a rich tone rings out and she gasps at the piano-tuner's skill. She's never had time to play the piano herself — it had seemed exclusively her brother's domain, while she had been busy helping her mother in the house. And then she'd married and given birth to four children in quick succession, and so it went, her life so full that she'd hardly noticed the passage of time until that day when the news came that Daniél, her firstborn, had been stabbed by his jealous wife. Daniél had been tall and handsome like his father, a boy beyond reproach, too good perhaps for this world. Mári carries his portrait in a locket between her breasts. Just as he had been laid on her belly moments after his birth, taking his first shuddering breath, he now lies eternally over her heart. It was God's mercy that her husband Hector had died first; he would not have been able to bear it.

She sits on the piano stool, smooths her skirt, and lays both hands on the keys, blessing them. With her left hand she touches the locket while with her right she ventures into a scale. Gabriela says it is too late for her mother to start messing with the piano, but Mári knows that it is never too late for an old dog to learn new tricks. "Do not conform to the pattern of this world, but be transformed by the renewing of your mind," she has read in Romans 12:2. In three days her teacher will come and she will take her first piano lesson. An unaccountable feeling of excitement rises in her breast until she can no longer suppress a burst of laughter.

Oriol and Osvaldo pass the night at Erminda's house where they sleep peacefully in *una cama matrimonial* covered with a flowered sheet and a ruffled counterpane. At breakfast they are instructed by Erminda's husband Nando who has already been to *la panadería* to buy fresh bread, and tells them once more how to find *la casa azul de* Yánis.

As they leave Erminda's house the rain begins. In Baracoa it can rain for days: torrential rain gushing from the mountains, swelling the rivers that clasp the town until they burst their banks, splashing down and down, sluicing the gutters, overflowing into every crack and corner, pooling around trunks and roots until all the vegetation is drenched, drunken, dizzy with excess. After tuning Yánis' piano in the front room of her blue house, as well as a third piano at a neighbour's house, they arrive at the bus terminal just in time to purchase tickets for their return trip to Guantánamo. Their clothes are dripping wet. Osvaldo takes his father's slippery hand and guides him up the steps of the bus. Oriol stands behind Osvaldo, places one hand on his sodden shoulder, and follows him down the aisle to their seats in the very back. The motor is already running, driving the air conditioning at full force and the old man begins to shiver in his thin shirt. There's nothing to be done. He must endure a frigid three-hour journey along the winding highway. As the huge wheels thrum and vibrate under him Oriol hears inside his head, though distantly, a swollen sound like rushing water which carries him out of his shivering body. He had the gift of sight for almost thirty-five years and has an archive of visual memory stored within. He conjures up the jungle landscape through which they travel, and when he tires of those lush vistas he turns to the movies playing in the darkness of his private cinema, old familiar scenes that Oriol never tires of watching, new stories that he creates from his own imagination, and sometimes disturbingly prescient images coming out of nowhere, unbidden and mysterious. But his senses are dominated by the soundtrack he composes to frame his visual memory. Sometimes it swells and envelopes him, carrying him over rapids on a turbulent river spilling into a whirlpool, dragging him under and spitting him out into the gasping air. At other times it is gentle, teasing, luring him deep into the jungle where each sound is so subtle that he has to strain to hear it. Oriol does not hear Osvaldo when he warns of their arrival. The return from his sovereign realm is always slow, leaving him as disoriented as one woken from a deep sleep, so he is surprised at being so suddenly summoned to walk once again down the aisle of the bus. But the warm touch and the smell of his son's skin brings him back to the present. Osvaldo takes his father's hand and places it upon his strong young shoulder. The old man could travel anywhere with his boy to guide him. They step down from the bus into shadow and enter the terminal, but when they emerge onto the main street he feels the comfort of warm sun on his face.

The rain hammers, driving Mári's little dog down from his rooftop patrol into the body of the house, where he crouches with ears laid back while Mári reads from Genesis about the Biblical flood that raged for forty days and forty nights. In Baracoa it rains only twenty-one days, but a relentless driving rain that leaves the town drenched and gurgling. On the twenty-second day the rain stops like a tap turned off and the sun comes out, causing the whole town to sparkle. But the damage is done. On the nineteenth day of the rains the ceiling over Mári's front room had begun to crack and crumble. She had immediately covered the piano with a large dust cloth which had somewhat protected the newly-tuned instrument from the plaster dust and falling debris when the final collapse had occurred, but could not prevent the soaking of the dust cloth and the inevitable entry of dampness into the old upright. She'd had no plastic sheet. Such things were hard to come by.

Alegra helps her grandmother with the paperwork necessary for the purchase of construction materials to repair the roof, and Yorki runs with the completed forms to Poder Popular. Various permits are required in the coming weeks, and Mári comforts herself with the thought that all that running will help to build Yorki's athletic muscles. Perhaps he will even travel outside Cuba someday to run for his country in the Olympic Games.

It is fortunate for Mári that she is well acquainted with the Bible and with the patience of Job, which to her is not a cliché but a lived experience, as it is to all Cubans of her generation who have been waiting more than fifty years for the Revolution's promise to bloom. Now she is to be tested in the cruellest way. Eight months after the collapse she still has not received her permits, though she has received advice from everyone on her street, some of whom have suffered similar damage and are caught in their own bureaucratic tangles. Mári has learned that even when permission comes the chances are slim of actually getting the cement, sand and gravel she has requested. Nor would it be much better to rebuild with corrugated roofing, as some have recommended, because the material would have to be ordered from La Habana which meant waiting a year or more. *Prima* Melvita has waited a year and a half to get batteries for her hearing aid and has in that time lost interest in what people are saying — even in the minister's sermons.

Alegra comes home with a new set of forms. 'The regulations have changed, *Abuela*. We must start over.'

Mári has already paid 357 pesos in registration fees, so her savings are severely depleted. She had hoped to accumulate a little for building materials but she's down to fifty pesos now, which will hardly buy a bag of cement. How will she afford another set of fees, and another visit from the piano-tuner when the renovations are complete? For she has not yet given up on her plan, though time is passing. She shuffles across the courtyard in her old house slippers, intending to sit on her bed at the back of the house and read her Bible quietly, but in mid-step something turns her abruptly towards the wreckage of the front room, as though she were a puppet. She surrenders to that force and finds herself standing before the shrouded piano. Someone guides her hand and lifts the dustsheet. The discoloured keys, with a gap between each, seem to smile up at her. Reymundo grinned like a demon, some had said, when he was under the influence of the rum bottle, but Mári had always seen the little boy behind that grin, the adventurous child who had taken refuge in his father's piano. She ventures once again to touch the keys and finds that the slightest pressure produces a rich sound that travels through her body, awakening the memory of Reymundo's playing. Her throat thickens. Sudden tears prick her eyes and fall between the keys, causing perhaps more damage to the instrument.

'An act of God,' she murmurs, pondering on the inundation that has changed her life as she realizes that the ceiling will perhaps never be restored in her lifetime, and that Alegra might go on a medical mission to Venezuela, and Yorki could become an international athlete. Then there would be no-one left to preserve the crumbling house. Mári begins to sing, a warbling hymn from their childhood — *'¡Despierta mi alma! Levanta tus ojos'* — to the force that guides her hand as she raises her unseeing eyes to the damage above her.

THE UNWELCOME GUEST

Onaldo had often talked about Rafael. They'd been schoolboys together in that same neighbourhood of La Playa, and Rafaelito had protected him from the school bullies, he'd said, so Karina was surprised to be greeted at the door by a small man — a bantam, though tough and wiry.

'¡*Feliz cumpleaños!*' she said, exchanging kisses with him, as was the custom. 'Sixty-five! *Un cumpleaños muy importante.* Now you will retire, no?'

'In Cuba there is no such thing as retirement,' he said, his blue eyes fixing on hers intensely. 'How can I survive on a government pension? No, no, no,' he wagged his finger at her, 'I must find more work — part-time jobs that will keep me running in all directions. It's not easy.' He gave Karina a knowing smile as he turned to embrace Onaldo, slapping him on the shoulder.

The front room was full of men, some seated on chairs arranged against the far wall while a couple were lounging against the door frame and still more were crowded into the back room where a ghetto blaster was pumping out salsa at top volume. Onaldo handed over the bottle of Havana Club that Karina had chosen. She didn't want to drink street rum, she'd told Onaldo, which was what the men were accustomed to, and which they were pouring now from large plastic pop bottles. The Havana Club was splashed generously into the waiting cups, even though some of the guests were already quite far gone. It was four in the afternoon on another steamy hot Baracoa day.

'This is our Canadian guest from Toronto,' Rafaelito said proudly as Karina smiled and shook hands with Francisco, Victor, Ángel, Manolito, Nelson, Rodolfo, Ulyses, Bismar, Yoel, Yurubí . . . They blinked at her, their eyes like camera shutters. It seemed she was the only female guest. When she asked about the other women she was led to the kitchen and introduced to a trio of cooks, one of them balancing a baby on her hip as she sliced tomatoes. The kitchen was a dingy affair with dark walls and a deep cement sink, but the women grinned at her cheerfully, and the young mother handed her baby to Karina while she finished slicing the tomatoes and started on an onion. The baby immediately grabbed Karina's necklace and tugged at it, gurgling with delight. She jiggled the child up and down, shifting from foot to foot, until the mother reclaimed him and thrust her plate of tomatoes into Karina's empty hands. The red slices glistened with oil and salt, wafer-thin slices of transparent white onion nestled on top, and a bent fork balanced on the edge of the plate. Onaldo took her hand and led her into the front room where the men were making yet another toast to Rafaelito. '*¡Feliz cumpleaños!*' they shouted in a slurred chorus. As soon as Karina entered the *sala* Rafael sprang forward and relieved her of the plate, insisting that she be the first to sample the bright tomatoes, so she picked up a slice with finger and thumb and dropped it into her mouth, raising her eyebrows as she savoured the red fruit. Rafaelito grinned and jogged his plastic cup against hers.

Onaldo took her hand again and led her forward. Immediately a skinny young man leapt up and offered his chair, hard and upright, in a row against the front wall. Bismar, a handsome old fellow, made his way across the room and sat next to her, leaning in to ask her opinion of Cuba.

'I love Cuba. Your Revolution is an example to the whole world of how to resist American imperialism. I am impressed by the loyalty of Cubans, how you help each other, how you manage to celebrate every occasion despite your difficulties, how you maintain a sense of family in the face of all the problems, how you love your children and share with your wives in the care of . . . '

From the corner of her eye she caught Onaldo's smirk. She had visited Cuba often enough to understand the agreed dialogue, reflecting back the clichés people liked to hear; a kind of non-dialogue, and one which Karina didn't mind since she was still focused on the language more than its content. Only when you knew someone well could you bring out your honest opinions; the complexities that sit better on a foundation of intimacy. She noticed Bismar's eyes glazing over as she told him about the time she'd heard Fidel and Chavez speaking in the Plaza de la Revolución in La Habana, then the rum bottle made a last round before it was drained, and all the men grinned and toasted Rafaelito as Onaldo snapped a couple of photographs.

It was at this point that Rafael's speech began to slur. He grabbed Karina's hand and repeated for the third time what a great friend Onaldo was, what a good man, how noble and intelligent, how admirable and honest. The word "honest" caused Onaldo to give Karina a sheepish grin. His lies and betrayals were legend — his attempts to extort money from her, his naivety in thinking she would fall for it because of her love for him. After several such incidents their relationship had ended and there'd been a period of bitterness and distrust before they'd arrived at a place of understanding which had ripened over time into genuine friendship as Karina had realized that Onaldo's betrayals had enabled her to clear some old emotional issues of her own that far predated him. It was okay. But Rafael's rambling repetition, his tugging at her arm as he spoke, not only irritated her but felt sentimental, even maudlin. Nothing more boring than a drunk, she thought. She raised a finger to Onaldo, with a slight lift of her eyebrows — their signal that she wanted to leave.

'But the food,' he said, hurrying to her side. '*Mi amor, tenemos a comer.*'

There was a pig roasting on a spit out back, and *las tres cocineras* were preparing rice and plátanos with malanga and huge platters of tomato and cucumber salad. Karina shrugged. Of course they couldn't leave without eating. Onaldo had been looking forward to the meal all day. Her attention was drawn to a woman standing in the doorway with a little girl hanging onto her and another hiding behind her skirt. She was a young woman with a kind of beauty that had been knocked askew, the main problem being that she had lost most of her teeth, although her lips were still full and sensual. She had a wounded though defiant look. Karina gestured to the seat beside her and the woman entered the house and moved forward eagerly to sit. Karina offered her own plastic cup of rum and the girl took it without hesitation. Her sip was a polite one — she didn't drain the cup — and she smiled with closed mouth as she handed it back. A low rumble of discontent travelled around the room as the two women began to converse. Though Onaldo sat contentedly at Karina's side, the other men in the room were clearly disapproving.

'*Me llamo* Hortensia,' she said. 'I live down the street with my mother and my daughters — they're twins.' The children still hovered in the doorway, too shy to enter but, after much encouragement from both Hortensia and Karina one of the girls launched herself at her mother and clung like a barnacle to her knee, while her twin continued to flirt from the doorway. Karina offered her cup once again and told Hortensia to keep it. She had a beautiful smile and dark green eyes with a quality of light like that reflecting off a sun-dappled pool. She spoke urgently of a broken marriage, another child who had chosen to stay with the father — 'He doesn't love me,' she said, almost whining.

'Your husband?'

'No, my *son*,' Hortensia insisted, as though the father were inconsequential. Karina wondered if the twins had a different father, as was the case in so many Cuban families, with multiple mothers and fathers and half-siblings.

'*¿Qué le pasó a tus dientes?*' Karina asked. It was impossible to ignore Hortensia's darkened mouth, filled with an emptiness that should come only to the elderly, though she did have a few molars in back, just enough to chew on. Without hesitation Hortensia launched into a story about her childhood in Matanzas where she had grown up sucking on sugar cane.

'It rotted my teeth,' she said, and pulled back the loose skin of her mouth to reveal a raw and ruddy darkness. 'Ah,' Karina nodded thoughtfully. It didn't sound quite right, but she decided not to pursue the matter further, then she couldn't help herself. 'Couldn't you get them fixed? It's free in Cuba, no? The dentist could make you some false teeth. *Eres joven.*' she insisted. '*Es una cuestión de salud.*' She noticed Hortensia glancing across the room, her eyes shifty and evasive, then Karina became aware of a man leaning against the far wall watching them. He was a serious looking guy with a heavy dark mustache — one of Rafael's friends to whom Karina had been introduced when she'd arrived, but the rum was getting to her. She couldn't remember his name.

Hortensia began talking too loudly, almost defiantly, as though she were showing off, but for whom? Was that her husband? Hortensia showed a strange mixture of defiance and cowardice in a kind of staccato rhythm, then suddenly the man lunged towards them and grabbed Hortensia's wrist. An involuntary whimper escaped her mouth as she pulled back cowering against Karina.

'*¿Qué quieres?*' Karina demanded, staring the man down, but he ignored her and continued pulling on Hortensia's arm as he spoke rapidly to her in a low hiss so that Karina couldn't quite catch what he was saying. Hortensia held her ground and refused to budge from the safety of the Canadian's side until Rafael came forward with a couple more of the men, menacing in their single-mindedness as they pulled Hortensia to her feet and, despite Karina's loud protest, dragged her towards the door. Onaldo, reluctant to involve himself in the altercation, began to caution Karina, but she was already on her feet babbling a torrent of adrenalin-driven words and phrases — ungrammatical, she realized as she heard the fractured Spanish coming out of her mouth, but she couldn't stop once she'd started. It was Rafael she addressed, demanding to know why they were harassing Hortensia. '*¿Porqué tu . . . tu permites a . . . a . . . a ellos acostar esta mujer?*' The men all sniggered, even Onaldo, some of them laughing out loud, and she realized she'd once more confused *acosar* with *acostar*, asking Rafael why they were putting Hortensia to bed instead of why they were accosting her. She and Onaldo would normally have a good laugh over her mistakes, but this time her stupid error only made her angrier. She knew that as a foreigner she didn't count. As far as they were concerned Hortensia was the only female at the fiesta apart from the three cooks who were safely in the kitchen where they belonged. With her gappy mouth and clingy children, her pleading eyes and her thirst for rum, Hortensia was destroying the myth.

'*¿Por qué ese hombre la empuja alrededor?*' she asked carefully. Why is he pushing her around?

'He's her brother. He has the right,' Rafael replied, thrusting out his chest.

The furious response on Karina's face threw Rafael into a panic. 'She's not welcome here! She must leave!' he barked, and now she could see how he had protected Onaldo. He was a scrapper. But he wasn't prepared to protect a *woman* against a bully.

'If she leaves I leave,' Karina said, pointing at the open doorway. 'You're brutes, all of you!' She registered the sudden concern on Rafael's face at the same moment that she felt Onaldo's hand on her shoulder, but she was already in motion, out the door and onto the street, on the edge of the scrum in which Hortensia, her brother and a couple more of the men were locked.

'She's your *sister!*' she shouted. 'Why are you treating her like this? *¡Es una ... una vergüenza! Ella es ... es ... es ... tu familia!*' Family — the magic word for Cubans, for what else did they have? She wanted to say so much more about the disgrace of it, the shame, but she was spluttering now and couldn't find the words. Besides which, Karina could see beneath the brother's mustache the thin twisted line of his lips, as though he might be winding up to hit someone. Not me, she thought, even as a snake of fear slithered through her. To hit a tourist would be a crime. He'd be sent to prison. The tourist, like the customer, is always right, because Cuba lives off tourism. She swung around as Onaldo took her arm and shook him off. Rafael stood in the doorway, trying to herd them back into the house, but Karina refused to move. She faced the brother full on and stared into his mean eyes, with so many thoughts racing through her head. She knew she was safe but what about Hortensia? Was she making more trouble for her? Was she acting like one of those ignorant foreigners who interfere in other people's business, who think they know better and try to impose their own values on another culture? Was she making herself complicit in all that oppressive colonial history? *'Por favor,'* she said with mock politeness, placing the flat of her hand on the brother's chest, keeping him at bay as she edged away slowly, taking hold of Hortensia with her other hand. In that same moment Hortensia shook herself free of the brother and latched onto Karina, her children still hanging onto her, round-eyed, with their sticky little mouths gaping open.

'*Vamos*,' Karina said, '*Ven adentro*,' and she reached for the hand of one of the twins. Hortensia had hold of the other child, and they moved as one body — hesitant and yet with a hint of pride on the face of the beaten mother as she settled herself next to Karina, smirking at her brother who glared still from the open doorway. It was he who stood on the outside now. How many punches to the mouth had she taken?

Soon the aroma of roast pig and steaming vegetables claimed everyone's attention, and Karina led Hortensia and the children to the kitchen where the cook, still holding her baby, gave Hortensia a plate piled high with food for her and the kids. They sat on a rickety wooden bench and ate ravenously. When they were done Hortensia grasped Karina's hands and kissed her on both cheeks, then she left with her little girls, their bellies tight like drums as they chanted in unison, '*Barriga llena, corazón contento*' — Full belly, happy heart.

Onaldo patted his belly and burped, satisfied at last by the meal he had come for. Already another giant pop bottle of street rum had appeared. Onaldo and Rafaelito would not discuss what had happened at the birthday fiesta. The matter would dissolve into the haze of the afternoon. Nor would the other men discuss it. Silence was best. In the end it had been a good meal with a few shots of rum to blur the edges of their difficult lives.

∾∾∾

LA ULTIMA PAELLA

for Roger Tro

Hipólito Hernando Aragón del Portillo was born a pale grub of an infant and grew into a dreamy child and a romancer. His head was filled with stories collaged from baby books, and he began to tell them as soon as he could speak. 'Mami! I saw a tiger on the beach chasing an elephant. And then . . . then . . . *mira* . . . a pirate came and chopped off its head with his *espada!*'

'*Mentira*, Popo!' his mother would exclaim, whomping his tiny bottom.

'No no no, Mami,' he said, shaking his little head. '*El pirata* came in a big boat, and . . . and . . . and it had cannons with *bocas de fuego*, they went bang bang! I had to cover my ears, Mami.'

'Lies, lies, you always tell me lies, Popo!' She wagged a cautionary finger at him. But the child was confused because he was only trying to share with his mother the dreams that illuminated his mind. Far from retreating into silence Hipólito insisted on his stories and invented elaborate structures to support them, and stubbornly repeated them day after day until his soft-hearted mother gave in. 'Ah, Popo,' she sighed, pressing his pale face to her bosom, 'My *muchacho* lives in his own world.'

His schoolmates were less indulgent, which made schooldays a torture until his retreat into the world of books. He learned to arrange his book-fed fantasies into credible scenarios, and won a scholarship to the university in Guantánamo and a second award for post-graduate studies in La Habana where he lodged in the house of Doña Lucía, who was an excellent cook, and where Hipólito tasted for the first time in his life *haute cuisine*. Every afternoon he would sit at the table with Doña Lucía and her pale daughter as he tucked into *ropa vieja* with creamy potatoes, *camarones con ajo y arroz blanco, pescado Santa Barbara, pollo frito y congrí* . . . Who knew where Doña Lucía managed to find the ingredients for these exotic dishes, and the delicate saffron to colour her rice? Indeed, when Hipólito told his fellow students of his gastronomical evenings they laughed at him. '*Ojalá!*' they guffawed. 'Don't you just wish, Aragón!' And they slapped him jovially on his broadening back. Everyone in La Habana called him by his surname, Aragón, so that was the name he adopted. It removed him from the memories of an awkward childhood and helped him to expand into a new persona. With the growth of his reputation as an historian a circle of influential academic colleagues began to surround Hipólito, just as his girth expanded to mirror his success (with the help of Doña Lucía's delicious meals), so that by the time he returned to live in Baracoa with his new wife, Yusmila, a fellow but lesser historian he had encountered in the stacks of the university library one feverish afternoon, Aragón was firmly and fleshily established with a new identity as a man of literal and metaphorical substance. It was as though a new person had come to town. No-one remembered Hipólito. He was Aragón now, lauded and respected as a Havana intellectual. He arrived home with three crates of books which he transferred one by one to the shelves of his new office at the Museo Matachín. His was the Office of the *Historiador de Baracoa*, because he was of course a Baracoan, even though absent for the past six years, and had returned triumphant with an accomplished though deferential wife who was already pregnant with a child who promised to be a son.

The Museum was housed in an old Spanish fort and was run by Osiris Rivero, a gentle archaeologist/anthropologist who housed there his discoveries from the wealth of Taíno remains surrounding the town. There were display cases filled with skeletons and pottery shards, stones inscribed with Taíno symbols, *caracoles, polymitas,* and many mysterious objects, the origins of which could only be speculated on. Sunk into the thick grass surrounding the museum were ancient canons pointing out above the sturdy stone wall, ready to defend the fortress from attack. But Rivero had not anticipated the kind of attack which was to strike at the heart of his museum.

Aragón sat silently plotting after dinner with his pregnant Yusmila, his own stomach as full and round as hers. His imagination worked on through the night, filling his dreams with an elaborate narrative, so that when he awoke sweating under the mosquito net he was tousled and flushed. After a shower and a breakfast of crusty bread with a ham and cheese *tortilla* and three cups of strong sweet *café con leche*, Aragón marched downtown in a crisp white shirt and his elegant sombrero to the offices of Adriano Barzaga, the Mayor of Baracoa, a man with whom he had already curried considerable favor by inviting him to his house for *pescado Santa Barbara*. It had been a jovial evening with many cups of Spanish wine and Havana Club consumed while Yusmila served the men, and Aragón carefully planted during the course of the evening a trench of false rumours about Rivero. With all the power of conviction that had enabled him to create his new persona, he managed to persuade Barzaga that Rivero should be removed along with his Taíno treasures, and relocated up the hill in Paraíso, where he could more readily display his bones in a cave. 'Quaint, no?' quipped Aragón. 'And Museo Matachín can be filled with *colonial* treasures — Spanish paintings, furniture and fabrics from the time of Diego Velasquez, the Governor of New Spain who made Baracoa his first seat of government and employed Hernando Cortés as Mayor,' he said with a flourish of his small soft hands. He leaned towards Barzaga and continued in an intimate tone, 'This is what our visitors want to see, not a collection of crumbling bones and *polymita* shells.'

The Mayor was convinced and Osiris Rivero, who at first refused the suggestion made to him, was ordered to decamp to El Paraíso where he did indeed set up a more genuine and site-specific museum, though unfortunately out of the way. Tourists from cooler climes were loath to climb the steep hill to the Paraíso caves in the steamy heat of a Baracoa day, nor did they favor the climb on rainy days when the hill became a stream of mud.

Aragón ensconced himself in his new office, surrounded by his books, and by a staff which included a tall and eccentric English speaker, the only one in town. Alben was to translate for Aragón during the evening presentations for tourists, held on the spongy green grass outside — which turned an eerie blue in the moonlight — amidst the sunken canons. Aragón was determinedly unilingual and, in any case, had a soft persuasive voice, while Alben's voice boomed above the sound of crashing waves on the nearby shore. El Museo Matachín was situated at the far end of the Malecón where the road curved past Playa Caribe, and doglegged left onto the road to Cabacú. In the park across from the museum stood an extraordinarily ugly statue of Cristóbal Colón, ironically placed in the firing line of the canons.

Yusmila did indeed give birth to a son and during her extended maternity leave Aragón — or, *mi pequeño* Hipo, as she called her husband, teasing him about his large spare tire — encouraged her to further expand her culinary horizons. 'I will try, *mi amor*,' she said, 'But Hipito, there is a limit to what one can make with rice, beans, and the occasional chicken leg. You know how difficult it is to find anything worth eating in Baracoa!'

Aragón was particularly fond of the food propaganda slides that were projected onto the wall of the Habanera Hotel on a Saturday night. He would take his evening stroll and linger there in front of the Hotel, munching on a cone of peanuts purchased from *el manisero*, rubbing shoulders with the likes of Yoel and Yurubí, ordinary working men. It was in one such moment, tipping the last peanut into his mouth, that he had a brilliant idea. He would travel into the countryside with Galina, the director of the Biblioteca, and a woman with remarkable knowledge of the local cuisine practised by the *campesinos*. He would invite Ricardo along with his little box camera, and together they would gather material — colour photographs, recipes, personal testimonies of *las cocineras tradicionales* — and he, Aragón, would publish it as a testament to his gastronomical passion and historical expertise, yes!

This was the first book and, though it was in fact a collage of everyone else's text and imagery, Aragón was credited with authorship because he had pulled it together; he was the *Historiador, un personaje,* a man about town and a magnet for the ambitious. Ordinary Cubans could not afford to buy his book so Aragón donated a copy to the Biblioteca where local people were free to go and salivate over the glossy photos of their very own traditional dishes before going home to the daily plate of rice and beans. Aragón bestowed upon Galina and Ricardo a copy each; he sent one to the Archbishop's residence in Guantánamo; and several copies to more influential acquaintances from his university days in La Habana. He displayed a copy in the lobby of the museum where it soon became grubby and dog-eared from tourists thumbing through it. The rest he hoarded in boxes in his office, with a copy strategically placed on his desk for all to see as they entered. His energetic sales pitch was for the most part lost on the Canadian, Italian, German, Japanese, Scandinavian and other assorted tourists who might have conversed with him in English had he mastered it. But one day a group of Spanish delegates arrived at the museum. They were important people from Madrid, on a cultural tour of Cuba, and had been referred to Aragón by their contacts at the university in La Habana. They loved the book, they loved the museum, they were charmed by Aragón and invited him to Spain on his own cultural tour. They carried back to Madrid half a dozen copies of his book — "La Comida Típica de Baracoa, Cuba," and they urged him to bring a couple of boxes when he embarked on his first trip to Spain.

Aragón had never before flown in an airplane, but as he was transported into the clouds with the powerful force of jet engines vibrating his nether regions, he felt strangely secure because it was, he realized, a familiar feeling. In his early flights of fancy he had accustomed himself to a sense of unfettered freedom and a belief in miracles, so he had no fear as he leaned back in his seat with a tattered grey belt straining at his belly and awaited his first beverage, which came with clinking ice cubes in a plastic glass complete with transparent twirler. His appetite was whetted by the cocktail, and when the meal arrived on a tiny tray which the hostess perched on the tiny table in front of him, Aragón tucked in with delight to each of the plastic containers with their salads, meats, potatoes and puddings, and licked them clean. If Aragón thought this was living he was in for a big surprise.

When he arrived in Madrid he was greeted by a buxom red-haired hostess who took him in a taxi directly to Hotel Catalonia Atocha, a luxury downtown establishment, close by, the *señorita* told him with a rise of one sculptured eyebrow, to El Prado, Museo Thyssen-Bornemisza, Palacio Reál and the Sabatini Gardens. 'What about your local cuisine?' Aragón inquired. 'This is my special area of interest.'

That night he was escorted to La Barraca where, his friends told him, he would experience the best *paella* in all of Madrid. And they were not kidding! Aragón's eyes popped as a gigantic cast iron pan was set on the table before him, sizzling with shrimp, mussels, squid, chicken, chorizo, peas and tomatoes, all jostling for purchase on a moist cloud of fragrant saffron rice. 'Ha! We can only *dream* of this in Cuba,' Aragón said, inhaling the aroma. '*¡Mi primera paella!* I am a virgin.' With these humble words he plunged the tines of his silver fork into a plump shrimp.

There were many more trips to Spain, and several more books, each one financing the next journey. The man who had trained as a historian became in fact more of a cultural commentator, though El Museo Matachín remained his calling card with its increasingly bored staff and its yellowing grass surround into which the canons sank centimetre by centimetre while Aragón grew fatter and fatter. With his corpulence came an increase in his reputation. Who in Cuba would question a man of such girth? Everyone knew that his belly signified success. 'All those trips to Spain!' they would exclaim, 'He's eating well, and they must give him money, look at his wife, she's a *gordita* too.' Beneath the tone of jealousy lurked a profound respect, for Aragón was one of their own, a *Baracoeso*. The towns-people felt they shared his success, if not with their bodies, then at least in their dreams. They loved to see him striding about town and barely noticed his declining mobility as he slowed to a waddle, then struggled with a cane, until one day the *manisero* asked, 'Where is Aragón? I haven't seen him on the street since Año Nuevo.'

'He must be in Spain,' answered Eugenia who, like Godofredo, was on the street every day, so she would know. 'He will be there,' she said confidently, 'eating *paella* for all of us. Give me a cone, Godo, I'm hungry,' she said, pretending to drop a coin into his *bolsa*, winking at him.

When Aragón thought of Spain it was indeed *paella* he lusted for. Business was good, in Madrid, Barcelona, Sevilla — he had travelled all over for many years and had sold hundreds, no thousands of his coffee table books to an ever-growing circle of Spanish colleagues and institutions — but in the end it was the food he travelled for and it was to La Barraca that he always returned, sometimes taking a taxi directly from the airport. He had tried all the best *paellas* in Madrid — at Casa de Valencia, at El Caldero, Alhambra, El Buscón, El Tigre . . . He had sampled *paella* at Bosque Palermo in Barcelona, at El Choto in Cordoba, at Paella Sevilla — but nothing matched that first sight of plumply naked shellfish, that first taste of spicy steamed mussels, that virgin experience of a completely satisfied gut filled with saffron rice and seafood. He had to return, just one more time, even though he could barely walk now. He booked his flight from Baracoa to La Habana, and from there directly to Madrid, and sent his son to pick up his tickets from the Havanatur office on Calle José Martí. When the day of his journey dawned he took a taxi from his house to the Gustavo Rizo airport where he had requested a wheelchair to transport him across the tarmac to the small plane that made the twice-weekly domestic flight north to La Habana. But there were no wheelchairs available and though the driver and his friends managed to extricate Aragón from the back of the taxi, over the curb, and through the airport building, they were unable to maneuver him across the wide expanse of tarmac to his waiting aircraft.

Hipólito looked up into a clear sky, the blue of his Spanish eyes disappearing into its expanse. Why couldn't he simply spread his wings and transport himself across the Atlantic, across Europe, and into his usual chair at La Barraca. His only desire now was for *la ultima paella*. 'Just one more, oh Mami grant me just one more, please . . . please . . . *por favor,* one more *paella* for your little Popo.

∾∾∾

December 18, 2014

Tito's face flushes with anger as he picks up the newspaper from the front step and sees the smug face of Raúl Castro staring up at him. Beside Castro, unbelievably, stands Obama with his mouth open in mid-speech, his hands raised in an earnest gesture.

AFTER HALF A CENTURY, A THAW IN U.S.-CUBA TIES, the headline reads.

Beads of sweat break out on Tito's wrinkled brow, but he can't help dredging up a phlegmy laugh when he sees the horns on Castro's forehead, drawn with a blue ballpoint pen! Despite his laughter a turmoil of emotions battle in his chest as he turns and lumbers towards the kitchen, his bare feet slapping heavily on the tiles. He throws the newspaper on the table, swallows a dyazide capsule and breathes deeply to calm himself as his doctor has instructed, then he turns on the television. Rubio is being interviewed on FOX News. Surely he must be outraged at this, Tito thinks, but no, Marco Rubio, ever the cool politician, maintains his calm exterior. 'Still trying to pass himself off as a presidential candidate,' Tito mutters to himself, 'But he doesn't have the balls it takes.'

Rubio has already served several years as a Republican junior state senator, gathering considerable support with his pro-life/climate-change-denial platform.

'The President has no right to take this executive action,' Rubio says in his infuriatingly mild manner. 'Neither the Senate nor Congress has approved his illegal action. As incoming chairman of the Senate Foreign Relations Committee's Western Hemisphere sub-committee, I will do everything in my power to block these reforms.'

'*¡Coño!* 'Tito explodes. 'Mario lacks charisma in spades. I could be listening to a prissy school marm! *¿Por qué no puede hablar como un verdadero Cubano, con pasión?*'

He slams the remote down and pads over to the kitchen counter to pour himself a second cup of coffee. Blanca is still asleep. Tito's always been an early riser, even during his childhood in Matanzas he'd be up and out playing before the household stirred — except for the *muchacha* who started work at dawn — and he would stare up at the rustling leaves of *las palmas reáles*, caressing their trunks with his little hands. His own kids are long gone, Eddie in Manhattan pursuing his career, Julia in upper state New York with that dumb-ass husband of hers, raising the *nietos*. It's just him and Blanca rattling around in their ranch-style bungalow. *Gracias a Diós* he has his work, his air-conditioned office to go to every day. But it's too early yet.

Tito spoons more sugar into his coffee. The blonde with the *tetas grandes* is wrapping up her interview with Rubio and faces the camera to announce that Republican Congresswoman Ileana Ros-Lehtinen is unavailable for a studio interview at this moment but she has commented over the telephone that

Obama may have broken several laws by acting unilaterally, including the Cuban Liberty and Democratic Solidarity Act of 1996, the Cuban Democracy Act of 1992, and the Trading with the Enemy Act. When FOX turns to sports Tito mutes the *chica*.

Gone are the days when he'd dreamed of a Cuban President for the United States. He used to believe in the possibility of a bilingual US with strong alliances between Florida and California — between Cuban and Mexican immigrants, Puerto Ricans and Guatemalans, Venezuelans, Bolivians, Chileans, Colombians and Hondurans . . . '*El español es el segundo idioma más hablado,*' he says aloud. 'Forty-five million Spanish speakers across this continent — and forty percent right here in Miami . . . ' he prods the kitchen table with his forefinger, 'where we have a rainbow of Latino immigrants. Thirty-seven percent in LA, thirty-six percent in San Antonio Texas, seventy-two percent in El Paso Texas, and . . . ' Yes, it is his old electorial dream-speech, and he would have given as an example Canada, a bilingual country despite the fact that only twenty-two percent speak French. He'd done his research even though Americans knew nothing about Canada except that it was covered in snow, causing the older inhabitants to escape to Florida, especially the Francophones, who are more or less close to the sunshine state.

Tito's eyes narrow as he imagines the wraparound effect on a broad map all along the southern frontier from coast to coast — California, Nevada, Utah, Arizona, New Mexico and Texas — states which used to belong to Mexico, as well as parts of Wyoming, Colorado, Oklahoma and Kansas. 'We deserve to run the country!' he booms, surprised at the force of his own voice in the early morning quietness of his shaded bungalow. 'We are Latinos,' he hunches, whispering to himself, 'the second largest language group in the world. And now look who we're governed by.' He slaps the open mouth of Obama on the front page. 'And look who's our only prospect —' he says, gesturing towards the TV screen where Rubio is mouthing silent words — 'Mario of the dynamic personality. *¡Coño!*'

When Tito opens up the newspaper to skim through the rhetoric of the Castro-Obama speeches his eye catches a sinister piece of information —

A U.S. delegation quietly travelled seven times to Canada in 2013 and 2014, coming for meetings that covered a swap of prisoners and the re-establishment of diplomatic relations. "I don't want to exaggerate Canada's role," the prime minister said, "We facilitated locations where the two countries could have a dialogue to explore ways of normalizing their relationship."

'*¡Mama huevo!*' That smug journalist must be laughing at him today. She'd been so inquisitive, *una inocente* with her wide blue eyes — Cuba? the embargo? the fate of Allan Gross and the Five? . . . She was probably a spy herself, probing him for details of CANF's agenda. *Claro* — he began to realize, she seemed to know a little too much about the Cuban American National Foundation — its beginnings in 1981, its affiliations, the office address and phone number — but they'd moved to new offices on Calle Ocho so she'd had to persist in order to find him.

'Your phones are not working,' she'd complained. 'The custodian at the old building redirected me, but I had to walk two and a half kilometres in this heat.'

And I was a *caballero*, Tito thought indignantly. I invited her into my office, offered her a glass of water, a comfortable chair.

'What do you think will come of this proposed exchange of prisoners?' she'd asked, 'Could it really happen, the release of Allan Gross in exchange for the remaining three of the Five Heroes?'

'Heroes?' he'd thundered. 'My god, those men are criminals, murderers!' And he'd explained it all to her, only yesterday. 'They were responsible for bringing down a Brothers to the Rescue plane in '96,' he'd said. 'Four innocent men killed trying to carry out a humanitarian quest! Those traitors will never see their freedom, especially not the ringleader. He's serving four life sentences.' It was all coming back to him now, like the memory of an oasis on a hot afternoon. The cool air of his freshly painted office . . . her big blue eyes . . . But he'd been fooled, that oasis was a mirage like you see in the movies, false pictures created by shimmering heatwaves. When she'd asked about *Las Damas de Blanco*, pretending to know nothing, he like a patsy had told her about Berta Solaire's visit to Miami for training in self-defence, about the ladies' peaceful protests all over Cuba, with their arms full of gladiolas. She pretended to be shocked when he'd told her about their imprisonment in Havana. And oh, how sneakily she had manoeuvred her way into his personal story.

Blanca's heavy footsteps — he feels their vibration — his hearing is not so good these days. He'll pour her coffee in a while. She always takes her time in the bathroom, showering, perfuming, beautifying herself for the day. First, he needs to settle his mind. His temples are throbbing. No more coffee for me, I'm already over my limit. One cup a day, the doctor said. If you must. In the morning. He sighs and stretches, fills a glass with filtered water and walks out to the back patio where a yellowing patch of grass is just beginning to receive the sun. It's early yet, but his wife is up and this historic day has begun. All around him the neighbourhood is awakening, he can feel it, the subtle sounds and movements. Soon the cars will be revving up and backing onto the streets, dogs barking and children yelling at each other on their way to school.

He had told that inquisitive *periodista* about his family's flight from Matanzas in 1962 after the nationalization of their land. 'We lost everything,' he said. 'Our land, the house, our money. You can't imagine the stress. Every night we lay in bed listening for a knock on the door. And when we reached Miami, we were waiting and waiting for Papi to come. I was fifteen years old, and I didn't know if I would ever see my father again.'

'Do you go back?'

'I will never return to Cuba. My life is here. I am a Cuban American.'

'But wouldn't you go back if the embargo ended? With papers you could reclaim your land.'

¡Coño! The devious bitch! She'd known even then as she'd asked the question. And he had admired her, not a *jovencita* certainly, but passably attractive — well-preserved, with an interesting accent, and *un perfume seductor* that had lingered on his shirt. He'd been completely taken in and that made

him even angrier than today's disastrous news. *¡Dios mío!* This changes everything. Tito doesn't know what to think. Obama can't end the embargo. A Republican-controlled Congress won't allow it. How were we to know that this uppity negro would turn into a dictator like Castro, taking matters into his own hands, bypassing Congress, the Senate, the House of Representatives?

'The so-called embargo means nothing,' he'd said, wagging his finger at that cunning blue-eyed fox. 'The Castros use it as an excuse for all their failures of government. They used it to get Soviet support, they blamed it for their so-called "Special Period," while the real problem is Fidel Castro and his stubborn pride. *He's* the one who closed the door. The truth is,' Tito remembers leaning across his desk into the cool breeze of his air-conditioner, 'The US is the biggest provider of food supplies to Cuba. But we don't give credit like Venezuela and those countries that want to invest in a communist regime with a disastrous history of human rights abuse. We demand cash.'

'And your property in Matanzas?'

'Impossible to reclaim, even with papers. The Castro regime will continue long after Fidel and Raúl are gone. Even now they're planting strategic leaders in government and industry. They've been very careful to train their acolytes in their own dictatorial ways. Our only hope is that the new generation, *without blood on their hands,*' he'd emphasized, 'will be . . . '
Her mouth was opening with yet another question, but Tito had — yes, he must have sensed something even then, his blood pressure rising, a warning, a sense perhaps that his words might be repeated somewhere, even in print — he had

stood up with an apology — his work, the recent move, so much to do, of course she understood. He'd stepped out from behind the fortress of his desk and kissed her on both cheeks, chastely of course, something to feed his fantasies . . .

Tito hears the murmur of the television. Ah, Blanca must be up and dressed, in the kitchen already. Just wait for it. She's watching the news, and she'll soon come running with an earful for him. He slumps into his sagging deckchair and closes his eyes, then it all comes flooding in — the sound of his mother's *chancletas* slapping the tiled floor as she bustles about the house, the sodden squelch of wet cloth as the *muchacha* washes their clothes in the *pila* on the back patio, the soft intimacy of Mamita's voice as she leans down to whisper to his father, and that glimpse of her breasts swinging loose inside her blouse. His body stirs with memory and, strangely, Tito feels close to tears. What is this? he wonders. I'm an old fool. The sound of rain pouring off the roof after a squall is so immediate that he opens his eyes, thinking it's real, but there's no rain, only another dry Miami day with a cloudless sky, still pale, yet to claim its colour. '*Maní, maní*,' he hears — the peanut vendor's voice in the distance . . . Tito's heart swells and he is a child again running downtown on Calle del Medio with a peso clutched in his hand, Mami calling after him, '*¡Tito, ven aquí, Tito, escuchame!*'

Blanca is calling him. He tries to answer but his constricted throat won't let him. Cuba, *mi* Cuba, *A solo 358 kilómetros de distancia*. Will I ever go back to my country? Yesterday he said a categorical no, but today everything is different. Who is he now? He's a Miami Cuban married thirty-six years to a Miami-born Cuban girl. He had married Blanca on her twenty-second birthday. *Qué hermosa chica, caliente al trote pero inocente.* They were a good match. But would she go with him? No. She'd never been to Cuba. It meant nothing to her. For Blanca Miami was Cuba. And the kids? True blue Americans, born and bred. They had nothing to look back on. When he spoke of his youth in Matanzas their eyes glazed over. Only forward, forward, that was all his son cared about — "going forward" — that stupid phrase parroted by all of corporate America — "Our company expects to make a profit *going forward*; We don't expect any layoffs going forward." *¿Qué diablos significa?* And what the hell will it mean to be a Miami Cuban if there's no more rift? I've built my career on that fault line, so have we all — Ros-Lehtinen, Rubio, Mario Díaz-Balart — and just about everyone on the Republican side in this state. What will we do now for our political and economic welfare? Obama has flouted the power of the Senate and the House of Representatives; he's dismissing the voice of our clan, us Cuban Americans.

Tito throws back his head and sighs. The sky is already a deeper blue, battling with the intensity of the sun as it rises towards its midday climax. How the elements mirror us, he thinks. Soon it will be evening and everything will darken and disappear into the night, except for the crescent of a new moon and the stars so very far away. We'll have to sit it out, he thinks, our time will come. But his next thought, rising like an alligator from the Zapata swamp, is that time is running out. Will I go home? he asks himself. Will I go back to Matanzas one more time?

୶୶୶୶

N ando goes twice a day to the *panadería*, plastic bag in hand, dawdling on the street to greet his neighbours, then stopping for a full minute to gaze up into a perfectly clear blue sky. Ah, the rains have washed the clouds away yet again. He inhales the freshness of the morning. An aroma of warm bread spurs him on to join the lineup in front of the bakery.

When he returns with his fresh bread, and a handful of ripe red tomatoes he encountered along the way, he closes the *portál* gate carefully behind him and turns to find Erminda anxiously waiting. 'Your coffee is ready. Where have you been? *¡Bandolero sin verguenza!*' she quips, remembering how they had carried on in their youth, a scrim of memory through which she still sees him, her handsome thirty-year-old bridegroom, and she a shy seventeen-year-old unable to believe her good fortune.

Nando was one of the men who built La Farola, sitting atop a giant excavator that cut through the jungle, dividing the mountains, tumbling the red earth into huge piles, crushing it, flattening it, shaping it to Fidel's wishes, all the while breathing thin air, perched high above a shifting landscape backed by

Biblical banks of cloud lit in the late afternoon by the golden ball of a sinking sun. Now he sits in front of his postage stamp TV watching a snowstorm of bad reception — *las noticias* three times a day, *la novela* — the soap opera — foreign films with Spanish subtitles, but most often, as Erminda scurries by in her *chancletas,* heading to the *portál* to gossip with her neighbours, Nando's eyelids are closed in a gentle sleep, his head erect, as though he were merely resting his cloudy eyes.

Beside the TV is a photo of their wedding — Erminda in first blossom, wearing a white dress, holding onto a man whose rakish looks and pencil-thin mustache are reminiscent of Clarke Gable. There is a belying cruelty to Fernando's thin-lipped grin, for he is in fact the gentlest of men. Inside his mottled skin lives yet that young man, his hand, now twisted with arthritis, resting on his bride's shoulder, claiming her. Erminda is more than a decade younger and can still dance circles around him, then she will stop suddenly and lay her head on his chest in a gesture beyond words. For almost sixty years they have been inseparable, retiring together each night to their marriage bed, Erminda's small body curved around Nando's back, shaping itself to him as though they were indeed the one flesh of which the Bible speaks. And they were joined psychically even when physically apart, for there had been times in the early days, the 1960s, when they had not seen each other for weeks on end because Nando was working on the construction of La Farola. Fidel Castro himself had authorized construction of the highway soon after the triumph of the Revolution, to join Baracoa to the rest of Cuba. La Farola had a life of its own, like a mythical serpent winding its way through the mountainous jungle above a tiny but powerfully historic town perched on the edge of the sea, divided and held and irrigated by a torrent of rivers that eventually, after all their flowing, gave themselves to the ocean.

It has been a long retirement and even after Nando turns ninety he continues puttering between his chair and the front *portál* where he leans against the balcony rail to observe the comings and goings on the street. He is *La Guardia* — a job he did throughout his long career as a construction worker and driver of heavy machinery, taking his night duty in stride when his turn came around, guarding the huge tractors with their mud-encrusted wheels. Pacing the *portál*, Nando thinks more and more on this, and on the many hours of his life that have passed in duty and in bone-shaking labour. He feels exhausted with it. '*Trabajando, trabajando,*' he mutters to himself, indicating the eternal nature of the work with a gesture of his hand, like a man scything grass in a field. He sits more and more in front of the television with its flashing pictures, but he has turned down the volume so that he can meditate more peacefully. Erminda fails to notice this because, being thirteen years younger than Nando, she is still on the move and is in any case a person of a quite different temperament. Sometimes Nando simply sits with his hands over his mouth and his eyes closed, like two in one of the three monkeys — *no ver el mal, no hablar mal* — though he *hears* everything that goes on in the house with its succession of comings and goings — the tourists who lodge in the back room with a door onto a patio bedecked with plants, his daughter and son and the grandchildren and great grandchildren who visit daily and sometimes several times a day, Erminda's many sisters and friends, and the vendors with eggs or bags of guavas or slices of cheese arrived fresh from Camagüey on the bus. There is a lot of traffic.

Nando has noticed that, since their return, the Heroes have become television stars, appearing on shows with scantily clad girls dancing around them, and singers at their side bellowing into microphones. Everyone wears a smile. Oh, how their faces must ache, he thinks. You can get *un dolor de cabeza* from smiling too much. It happened to him on his ninetieth birthday and Erminda had to massage the back of his neck and give him one of her Ibuprofen pills. Gerardo, Antonio, Ramón — they look much older now, but they are *gordos* — how can that be after so many years on a prison diet? The Yanqui spy, after only five years in a Havana jail, looks old and wasted, Nando observes, and he's lost a lot of teeth. Erminda has told him that Gerardo's wife is to have their baby early in the new year.' *Pero es imposible,'* he said, 'He's only been home since mid-December.' Erminda explained to him about artificial insemination, but Nando is troubled by such things and finds it better to simply mute the sound and close his eyes.

One day, after a particularly heavy meal, served to him in the heat of midday, Nando feels horribly nauseous. He retires to the bathroom and tries to hawk up his lunch, without success. He sits on the edge of the toilet with his head in his hands for so long that Erminda raps at the door — 'Nando, are you all right? *¿Qué está pasando allí?'* The sounds have alarmed her because Nando has never been a man to make such a rumpus in the bathroom. Admittedly in recent years he has begun to snore and fart in his sleep like an old dog and Erminda has to nudge him hard and sometimes even take an extra sleeping pill, but these noises behind the closed door sound more serious. She helps him to the bedroom and lays him down with a couple of lumpy pillows to support his head. She presses liquids on him — orange juice, milk with sugar and chocolate powder, tea brewed with *manzanilla* leaves from her plant on the back patio. He wants none of it. He has to vomit. There is no alternative.

Laura arrives from her house around the corner. 'Papi, you have to drink,' she insists, echoing her mother as they hover above him. Finally he manages to stagger to the bathroom and vomit, and then he lies down again, feeling better, but he continues his rebellious fast for two days in which time his left leg swells up, and an old hernia in his groin revives, causing a painful and embarrassing swelling. 'You have to keep your leg up,' Erminda says. '*Vamos*, Nando. *Levántate de la cama.* Sit in the *balánce.*' She drags another chair from the *sala* to elevate his leg, and hurries to the kitchen for an ice pack.

Nando discovers the rocking chair to be surprisingly soothing once he is settled in it. From the corner of the bedroom he has shared with Erminda for so many years he gains a new perspective. He has never sat in this room before, except briefly on the edge of the bed to put on his socks and shoes, bending to tie them, more and more slowly with the years in order to avoid that dizziness that comes when he lifts his head too quickly. He forgives Erminda for her strident demands. Behind the urge to eat the food she has so painstakingly prepared for him he detects an edge of hysteria. She's worried about him, just as he had worried about her when her sister died suddenly in the summer and Erminda had taken to her bed with a dizzy spell and refused to consume anything but water. The other sisters had been tending her when Nando had opened the door a crack to plead with her — '*No te vayas, Erminda*' — Don't go. Don't leave me. *No te vayas.* What a prize she was, the most beautiful girl he had ever seen. And still when he looks at her this is who he sees — a seventeen-year-old with an air of mixed docility and wildness, her heart-shaped face framed with dark hair, her deep brown eyes so full of passion. He had tamed her and elicited from her all the joys and promises of her beauty.

For five days Nando does not venture from the bedroom, then one evening he surprises his wife by shuffling across the living room to watch the Heroes with her. Little by little he resumes his old habits until he is once more posted in front of the silent television at seven in the morning drinking his *café con leche* and chewing on a piece of fresh bread. Not so very long ago, it seems to him, he was out on the street early each morning to fetch bread from the bakery, to look for some meat for the midday meal, to greet his neighbours who were out on similar quests. But something is different now. It is like a dance, Nando thinks, this slow change that is claiming him. He is captive now to a force much stronger than any he has known during his long life. Erminda is constantly at his side, tending his still-swollen leg, smoothing the few hairs left on his head. He feels like an old rooster in a chicken coop with all the hens gone but one, and she is his queen.

'*No te vayas*,' she says, teasing him. '*¡Bandolero sin verguenza!*' And she swipes him on the side of his head in that rough way she has that hides her caring when it is too much for her.

'What has become of Fidel?' Nando asks as he chuckles and closes his eyes. He never sees him on the television screen these days, only the three *gordos* with their shining white teeth. Fidel has been silent a long time, Nando thinks. Perhaps he has died and no-one has told me.

N o-one ever forgot Godofredo's birthday. He was born on January 8th 1959, the day that Fidel Castro rolled into Havana atop a tank when his Revolutionaries had taken the entire country and Fulgencio Batista had fled to the Dominican Republic, en route to Portugal. Godo was fêted annually with cake and *refrescos* and with the congratulations of friends and neighbours filled with national pride as well as good wishes for the boy's birthday. Their felicitations were expressed more fervently with each passing year as their hopes for the Revolution grew until, in 1977, the sixteenth year of the American embargo, with Cuba's economic relationship to Russia still firmly in place, two incidents changed forever the course of Godo's life.

He was an unusually intelligent student, and had been encouraged early in his schooldays to pursue a career in the sciences. In fact he could have pursued any career he wished, because he was talented in almost everything, from mathematics and science, to languages, the arts, and the social sciences. His mother Liliana, a fervent though necessarily clandestine Catholic after the Revolution, harboured a desire for her only son to become a priest, but her husband Alfredo persuaded her that this would be a criminal waste of the boy's intelligence, even if religious practices were to become legal in time. Alfredo had in any case no time for the church. He'd never had much time for the Revolution either after he'd seen what followed the triumph. He harboured his anti-revolutionary feelings secretly, keeping a low profile with his neighbours, and with colleagues at the bank where he measured out his days in deposit slips. His greatest desire was to give voice to his opinions and to gather a following as a dissident leader but, though he found it easy to criticize, Alfredo was not an original thinker and could conjure up no fresh ideas on national governance. Instead of speaking out, which would have taken him straight to prison, he began to accumulate a nest egg of American dollars, slowly and carefully garnered in the course of his daily work. After hours, in the privacy of his teller's cage, he would handle the sensuous green papers and think of all the hands they had passed through on the streets of Miami where dollars travelled from one store to another, from bank to bar to restaurant, perhaps even passing briefly through the hands of John F. Kennedy himself, or Lyndon B. Johnson who had succeeded him. Alfredo would not have called his practice embezzlement; he felt on the contrary that it was essential to his self-esteem and was the only thing that prevented him from drowning in the despair of the daily tedium that was his life.

Godofredo had just turned eighteen and was to enter university in Guantánamo when the catastrophe occurred. He was in Mayajara, at his uncle's *finca* with big sister Marisel. It was from there, high in the jungle, his uncle had told him, that the Taíno Indians had first sighted the galleons that signalled the arrival of the tall white strangers — Columbus and his conquistadors, who thought they had arrived in Paradise, and planted their cross firmly in the sands of Baracoa. That cross had survived and had been authenticated by European carbon dating experts as the original *Cruz de la Parra*. Later, much later, Godo would see it for himself, displayed behind glass in the Catholic Church, and he would stand staring at it, wondering at its perfect preservation after five centuries.

Tío Ernesto's *finca* was rich with coconut palms and mango trees. It was August and the ground was covered with fallen fruit. Even the ants staggered drunkenly over sticky mango skins, supping from their sweet wounds. Godo shinned up a coconut palm with a machete swinging from his belt, and as he climbed he imagined how the coconuts would go tumbling to the ground and how they would spurt like pop bottles as he chopped into them, slicing their heads off, handing them to Marisel and Tío Ernesto to drink the sweet water that would drizzle down their chins and onto their necks, cooling them. As he reached the top he was temporarily blinded by a ray of sun which pierced the leaves, so that he had to switch his angle and find a firm foothold a few inches to the left. Securing his position, he reached with his machete and aimed it carefully at the cord that held the coconuts, with exactly the right amount of force, as his uncle had taught him. But his left hand slithered and he lost his grip just as the machete struck home. Suddenly he was tumbling — turning and circling in the green air — his breath suspended until he hit the ground. There was a moment of complete silence before he heard Marisel's scream and with it came an excruciating pain. When he looked down he saw no blood, only the protrusions of several splintered bones in his right ankle and, when they lifted him, the useless dangling of his foot as though it were separate from his body, a puppet suspended by wormlike tendons. He heard a scream, like a pig being slaughtered, before he passed out.

He awoke in a strange bed struggling to return from a dark place he could not remember. There was a strong antiseptic smell. As soon as he tried to move sweat broke out on his upper lip where a soft moustache was beginning to grow, and when he tried to get out of bed he realized that he was hobbled. His right leg was encased in plaster from his toes to his knee. He fell back and sank again into a deep sleep.

Godofredo remained in the Guantánamo General Hospital for many months, enduring multiple operations on his shattered ankle. When he was eventually transferred to Baracoa, bouncing along the newly built La Farola highway in an ambulance, there was a tearful reunion with his mother who had been unable to visit him for lack of funds. 'No te preocupes, mi hijo,' she said. 'You will have your career. I will find a wheelchair and you will attend classes at the university.' But it would be two more years before Godo could even stand, let alone think of resuming a normal life. And in that time his father made a fatal error. Distraught over his son's accident, Alfredo began to accelerate his operation, branching out into the illegal sale of American dollars. It seemed safe enough. There was any number of currency sales on the street, negotiated by men with little to lose. But Alfredo had much to lose. He was a man of reputation. He had never caused any trouble. He never complained. He was completely trustworthy as far as the Bank was concerned. So, when the news came that Alfredo had been caught by the police everyone felt betrayed.

'There's little enough in life that we can trust these days,' said a fellow teller, flashing her manicured nails in the air. 'But Alfredo? Who would ever have suspected him?' She was outraged. The neighbours were outraged. The entire town of Baracoa was up in arms.

Alfredo received a quick sentence of ten years imprisonment with the additional punishment of not being able to see his family, because he was to be transported far away to Matanzas, almost the entire length of the island. But worst of all was the shame. The family was shunned. Only a few faithful neighbours visited with Liliana late at night, commiserating in low voices. '*Ay Chica, que cosa,*' Pucha whispered as she leaned across from the next-door balcony. 'What will happen now to Godofredo? *Que lastima,* such an intelligent boy. *Que vergüenza.* He won't be accepted now at the university,' she said, shaking her head sadly.

Godo's career began by coincidence. Pucha happened to have a cousin who brought freshly roasted peanuts from Guantánamo twice a week to sell on the street, and he needed someone to fashion twist cones from old newspaper pages and fill them with nuts. 'The *muchacho* who used to do it has got himself a job in the chocolate factory,' Pucha explained. 'I asked my cousin and he wouldn't mind if Godo did the job. It's easy work, he can sit at the table in his wheelchair no problem. One peso for one hundred cones.'

Liliana swallowed the last fragment of her pride and accepted on behalf of her son. While Godo worked she sat by his side and read the Bible to him in a low voice so as not to attract attention. But she need not have worried. One of the benefits of banishment, they learned, is that it makes you invisible.

Godofredo was already twenty-seven years old and sporting a splendid moustache when he inherited the role of *Manisero de Baracoa*. His sister Marisel, who was by then married with two little boys, took over the job of cone-making and Godo took to the streets, limping but ambulant. The family's shame was long forgotten and, in any case, Godo was not recognized since he had been so long in the house making cones or else at the polyclinic undergoing physiotherapy to strengthen his foot and ankle. Everyone bought peanuts. It was an impersonal business for the most part, though a few curious souls passed the time of day with Godo and asked if he was new to Baracoa. It was a fresh beginning and Godo welcomed it. I've served my apprenticeship at the kitchen table, he thought, now I'm out in the world and I'm going to consume it!

His father, much weakened by hunger strikes, came home a broken man after serving his sentence. To be greeted with the news that his only son had become Baracoa's peanut vendor did him no good. He died shortly after his homecoming, to the relief of Liliana who no longer recognized the passionate young man she had married.

ᘖᘖᘖ

December 2014.

Godofredo wakes to the sound of Jose Feliciano — '*Feliz Navidad, Feliz Navidad, Feliz Navidad, Prospero año y felicidad . . .*' He swings his legs over the edge of the bed and sits upright, feeling the floor tentatively with his right foot, as has been his habit since the accident. When he feels confident he stands up and limps barefoot into the kitchen to start brewing his morning coffee. It is seven o'clock and already sticky with what promises to be another hot humid day with tourists arriving in busloads for the Christmas season, not that Christmas is a big event in Cuba. It's New Year that draws the foreigners, anxious to celebrate yet another anniversary of the Revolution — fifty-six years, Godo thinks with a wry smile, a true child of the Revolution, getting old.

He heard a couple of gringas on the street yesterday talking in their stumbling Spanish to a group of *muchachos*. 'We're so glad we came *now*! It's all going to change so fast now that Raúl has shaken hands with Obama.'

'Yes, the embargo will be lifted and all the Yankee corporations will come in and *spoil* everything!' said the other girl.

Godo shrugs, with a dismissive gesture to his empty kitchen. The radio has told him that the remaining three of *Los Cinco Heroes* have come home after sixteen years in an American jail, exchanged for an American spy who served only five years and a CIA Yanqui who survived twenty years in a Cuban jail. Godo feels sick at the mention of prison sentences. '*¡Humanidad!*' he exclaims aloud, remembering José Martí's phrase, '*¡Patria es humanidad!*' It has always seemed to him that imprisonment is the worst kind of inhumanity. Better to die than to rot in captivity. He remembers the gaunt grey creature who came back from Matanzas, how he failed to recognize him as his own father, and how guilty he'd felt without quite knowing why.

He takes the coffee pot off the burner as it begins to bubble and shuffles back to his bedroom, noting with his left foot, the one that still has feeling, that the floor needs sweeping. A Cuban version of Jingle Bells is playing now and as it trails off there is the sound of kissing. The staff of the radio station are sending kisses over the airwaves to their relatives in Santa Clara, Camagüey, Pinar del Río, Cienfuegos . . . Godo wishes that his sister was with him instead of in Guantánamo with her daughter-in-law and the grandchildren. Now that Marisel is retired she spends most of her time over there, and Godo is alone, cooking for himself, trying to keep the place clean and tidy. The corners of his mouth turn down and his eyes mist as he recalls the family Christmases when his parents were still alive. Even when his father was gone to Matanzas there had still been an attempt at celebration for *La Noche Buena* as his mother had called Christmas Eve. There was always a family meal followed by a reading from the well-thumbed Bible she kept hidden beneath her thin mattress. What joy in December '97 when Christmas was reinstated as a national holiday in honour of the Pope's imminent visit! With the ban on Christmas decorations lifted, Liliana had set up a modest crèche in the *sala*, and on *La Noche Buena* she had proudly entered Nuestra Señora de la Asunción with Godofredo at her side, and there they had prayed for his broken foot, though it was by then already much healed, leaving him with only a limp and the nightly cramps in his leg.

'*Baracoa ciudad primada, en los colores de libertad,*' sings the daily jingle in a syrupy little-girl voice. He's on the children's channel. Godo turns the crackling knob until he comes to *Radio Reloj* with its reliable ticking and regular news updates. 'Cuba in this 56th year of *Rrrevolución* . . . ' booms a deep voice. Godo sighs. I must listen either to children's jingles, he thinks, or to very old news of the youthful activities of men who are now very old. He had watched television the previous night after returning late from his beat in Parque Central, his jingling *bolsa* heavy with pesos. They had replayed the old film clip of a proudly bearded Fidel in army fatigues entering Havana with Camilo Cienfuegos at his side, tall and handsome. The clip was so familiar that Godo didn't even see it, like the time his papá had shaved his moustache and Godo hadn't noticed. Familiarity is a blindness, he thinks, remembering the months in hospital with his eyes closed against the pain. It is a foreign country of eternal repetition until you learn submission and become the servant. He had grown up with images of military triumph, but what was it like, he wonders, for those who had lived before the Revolution? And for those who came after, much later, only to learn about it in school? And what of Fidel? Everyone wonders at his silence as Gerardo, Ramón, and Tony return to Cuba. Is he too ill to speak? Is he even alive? Is he keeping silence until he's ready for one of his marathon speeches? Or perhaps he's angry about the new relation between Cuba and the US? Some say that the old Cuban-Miami families, the ones who fled after the Revolution, are still full of bitterness, holding onto their grudges and waiting to reclaim their property after more than half a century. Will Fidel face on his deathbed the mirror of his own rigidity in the form of the Miami right wing? Godo mulls over these questions as he prepares for yet another day on the streets of Baracoa, filling the old cloth *bolsa* with peanut cones, looping it over his shoulder. He stands a few moments listening to *Für Elise,* one of his favourites and an especially welcome relief in this season. As the final notes die away he switches off the radio and allows his thoughts to return to Christmas and how it will soon be over, then he can listen to Polo Montañez singing *Amenece el Año Nuevo* — on the radio, on the streets, in the bars. What a tragedy that our most popular singer died in a drunken car crash, Godo thinks. If Polo hadn't been discovered he would still be a *campesino,* singing to his oxen in the fields of Pinar del Rio.

The first person Godo greets as he strolls on the newly constructed Boulevard fronting Casa Cultural and Hotel Habanera is Heike, the German girl who comes back to Baracoa every year to visit her lover. She runs over waving merrily and greets Godo in her strange Spanish. *'Mein Freund, cómo estás?'* she lilts.

'Tan gorda!' Godo says with a grin, and then he sees her face fall. *'Tan gorda, tan gorda,'* he repeats, *'muy linda, mas joven que antes . . . '* — all the compliments he can think of, but she still looks offended, sucking in her stomach and pulling herself upright so that her breasts rise impressively. Godo thrusts a fistful of peanut cones at her. *'No quiero,'* she says, *'no quiero a engordarme.'*

'No te ofendas,' he says quickly. 'It's beautiful to be fat, Heike, a sign of prosperity, *la vida buena . . . '* But she's turned away, her attention caught by another German, a really fat one. Heike is in fact quite slim apart from her impressive breasts. Obviously she doesn't understand about the accumulation of flesh against an uncertain future. Godo remembers only too well the collapse of the Soviet Union and Fidel's "Special

Period," when everyone went to bed hungry, awoke hungry, perhaps managed a cup of watery coffee, and spent all day searching for food. There were even rumours that some ate the vital organs of corpses if they were lucky enough to work in a *funeraria*, or had money enough to buy the illegal meat. Many actually died of starvation. But nobody talks about that. They just say with well-meaning admiration, 'You're fat!' because that's how everyone wants to be. Godo remembered his sister so thin that she'd had no milk in her shrivelled breasts to feed her baby. And people's feet had troubled them, young and old, because there were no proper shoes. Godo was content to go barefoot because it was easier on his damaged foot, but he'd cut up old rubber tires to make shoes for Marisel and Liliana, attaching them to their feet with twine, which made them waddle like ducks. In the Special Period he had not been the only lame one.

Three days later Heike hails Godo on the street and after a brief exchange of greetings launches into her complaint about the lack of money in the Bank. '¿*Que voy a hacer?*' she asks. 'First there is no connection for my credit card, then the ATM eats my card, I have to go all the way to Guantánamo for a replacement and travel back to Baracoa in a cattle car with *campesinos* and their pigs and chickens! Now there is no money, neither in the Banco de Credito y Comercio, nor in La Cadeca. They have to send to Guantánamo for more convertible pesos. I'm so stressed with all these I feel sick to my stomach!'

Godo shakes his head sympathetically and offers her a couple of cones filled with fresh peanuts still warm from their roasting, and she accepts, pouring them into her mouth and chewing hungrily. 'Adolfo doesn't believe me,' she complains. 'He's waiting for money for our bathroom tiles and if it doesn't come soon someone else will buy them.' Godo pats her shoulder in an attempt to cheer her, and indeed her face brightens. 'Adolfo is building a *casa* for us in Cabacú,' she says proudly, smoothing the orbs of her breasts in a distinctly Cuban gesture. More likely feathering the nest for his *guajira,* Godo thinks. He has no faith in these relationships with foreigners. He's seen too many lovers' fights on the street, ending in the tears and tantrums of disappointed girls. Ah well, they pay for their adventures, he thinks, smiling apologetically at Heike. He'd like to warn her but he keeps his opinions to himself. People never listen anyway. They must learn for themselves. And who knows what the real lesson is? Perhaps it has nothing to do with the matter at hand. During his time in the darkness of the Guantánamo hospital, drugged to the gills with his eyeballs rolled back into his skull, Godofredo had discovered another reality which he likes to think of as *el otro mundo* of which Martí wrote. My discovery was possible only because of my accident, Godo thinks, and he is truly grateful despite the months of pain he endured and the sad redirection of his life. What if I had become a doctor? he often asks himself. I would have been working long hours at the hospital or at the polyclinic, writing prescriptions for all the sick people of Baracoa and earning at most twenty convertible pesos a month. And look at me — I have the freedom to walk the streets of Baracoa all day long. Everybody knows me and yet I am invisible because they see only *el manisero* and they expect no more of me than a cone of peanuts, the time of day, a word or two about the daily struggle. He does in fact harbour a strong desire to become a writer. This is his secret identity, and he sees his daily work as research. He knows from conversations with the local writer, Oscar Pérez, how easy it is to become addicted to research and to procrastinate over the actual writing process. So now he sees himself as a man who, though he never writes a word, carries a library of information in his head, awaiting the right moment.

Next day Heike sidles up to Godo with a big smile on her face. 'The convertible pesos have arrived from Guantánamo,' she says, 'I can have three hundred a day from the ATM.'

'¡Caramba!' exclaims Godo, his eyebrows shooting up. That was more than he made in two years. And it would all go on tiles for her boyfriend's bathroom. Perhaps I should set myself up as a *jinetero*, he thinks with a chuckle.

'What's so funny?' Heike asks.

'¡Felicidades! Estoy tan feliz!'

'*Gracias*,' she says, and with a little frown, 'It's still very stressful. Every time I put my card into the ATM I'm holding my breath in case the machine eats it and I have to take that trip to Guantánamo again across La Farola, which makes me dizzy with all the twists and turns.'

'You could go with your boyfriend on his motorbike. *¡Pelo suelto y carretera!*' Godo tosses his head in a gesture of abandonment, imagining Heike's blonde hair streaming behind her in the wind as she locks her arms around her lover's muscular torso, both their bodies vibrating with the thrum of the motor.

'Adolfo's bike is broken,' she says, the fine lines of a frown marring her milky forehead. 'He's waiting already two month for a mechanical part to come from La Habana. It's so boring to be every day in Baracoa. We used to travel many places — Playa Maguana, Parque Humboldt, Finca Duaba . . . ' Her voice trails off and she sighs, causing her breasts to rise dramatically and then sag with her exhalation as though her shoulders could not support their weight. Godo flushes and extends a handful of *maní* to her, which Heike accepts with a wan smile, leaning forward to kiss his cheek. Godo is so affected by the touch of her skin on his that he turns away in confusion just as Aragón, the portly city historian, passes by resplendent in a white *guayabera* with embroidered front and crisp cuffs. He wears his signature sombrero which he does not trouble to lift as he says in his soft nasal voice, *'Buenas tardes, manisero.'* Aragón drops a coin into Godo's bag, takes a cone of peanuts and inhales their aroma. *'Mmm, tan delicioso,'* he says and pours them into his mouth. Aragón has a slight lisp, Godo notes. Must be all his trips to Spain. Many of the Spanish tourists have the same lisp. When he turns back Heike is gone.

Godofredo has not been lucky with women. He'd had his eye on a girl in high school, but after the accident he never saw her again, though there had been one *chica,* a neighbour's daughter, who used to visit him in the evenings. Mercedes would stand at the door twisting her fingers, as shy as Godo. *'¿Cómo está tu mamá?'* she would ask.

'Mas o menos, mas o menos,' he would say. Okay, not too bad. Godo had been encouraged by her visits and by the fresh aroma surrounding Mercedes. He had only to close his eyes and the smell of her would fill his nostrils and arouse in him an intensity of feeling. He had been working up his courage for a kiss when his mother fell seriously ill. Liliana was in the

hospital only three days before she died. In no time, it seemed, she was dead and buried. Her body was laid out at the *funeraria* in the morning and at two in the afternoon they slid her coffin into the hearse and made the slow journey with it up the hill to the cemetery, Godo limping along behind with a spray of coral *isora* in his arms. There had been a few mourners to join him and Marisel — Pucha, some neighbours with their snotty children trailing along, and of course Mercedes. What made Godo sadder than anything was the fact that his mother had died without ever really living, though he supposed there had been happier times before his birth, before the Revolution — a time that he could only imagine. Liliana had never spoken of the past, and now it was too late.

After the death Mercedes had stopped coming to his door. It was unseemly for a Cuban girl to visit a young man alone in his home. Inquiring after his mother's health had been her only excuse. A few months later Godo had heard that Mercedes was to be married to a medical student from Guantánamo. 'They're waiting until he graduates,' a neighbour informed him, then she will move to Guantánamo. 'What good fortune to marry a doctor! And who would have thought it of such a quiet unassuming girl?' But what a body, Godo had thought, trying to distract himself from an emerging pattern of loss — first his career, then his papá, his mother, and now Mercedes. He had begun ogling the schoolgirls as they strutted around Parque Central in their skin-tight shorts and low-cut tops. He would make sidelong glances, trying to hide the evidence of his lustful thoughts. And alone in his bed at night he had fantasized about those girls and about their particularly alluring parts so that he didn't have to think about Mercedes and her imminent departure to Guantánamo.

It is six o'clock in the evening, the hour on the equator when the trees are alive with birds and the streets are crowded with a quick bustling of tired people unwinding after a long day, hurrying home, stopping only to buy bread or vegetables for the evening meal, crowding the doorways of stores for one last look before they close. It is the hour when a poor town can luxuriate in the end of the workday as it is crowned by the glory of a rapid sunset.

Godo turns down Calle Ruber López on his way home to rest before the evening which is when he makes his best sales, to tourists, hungry after guzzling half a dozen *Bucaneros*, or a bottle of Havana Club. He starts down the hill and passes a group of big ladies exercising in the street. They are clustered on the shady side facing a slim *chica* in magenta tights and yellow top. She jumps up and down, her arms flapping like birds' wings. '*Y uno y dos y un dos tres*,' she chants rhythmically, brilliant in the sunlight. Then she is suddenly eclipsed, her bright clothing losing its glow as the sun drops behind the buildings.

'*En tus manos, en tus manos, en tus manos Señor, en tus manos* . . . ' Godo hears the children singing as he passes the Pentecostal Church, a large blue building, newly renovated and still awaiting its finishing touches. Nothing is ever quite finished in Baracoa. He wonders if it's the same in La Habana. He's never been to the capital, but the tourists tell him that Baracoa is another country, a unique place, so he can only imagine what it is like outside. Now they're singing in a strange tongue, but he understands because it's the same tune. On and on it goes. Pablito has told him that they learn the same song in French, Italian, English and Portuguese. Pablito is six years old and very intelligent. He hops around Godo pretending to be a frog in his brand-new running shoes which are way too big for him and contribute, with his protruding eyes, to a froggy appearance. His mother has bought the shoes for him for *Año Nuevo* with money she's earned cleaning houses and cooking for a tourist B & B. She has made sure that there is room for Pablito's feet to grow.

Godo sometimes goes to the Pentecostal service on a Sunday morning when there's no business on the street with everyone either in church or sleeping after a night of fiesta and *amor*, raising their heavy heads only to blink at the light seeping in through the blinds, then rolling over for another half hour of shut-eye. Last Sunday, after a couple of rousing hymns accompanied by the Pentecostal band, with drums, saxophone, guitar and keyboards, the pastor had delivered an hour and a half of Biblical instruction. After listening intently Godo had come to the conclusion that the pastor was rather full of himself. He had created an argument with Immanuel Kant on the subject of egoism and identity, accompanied by a slide show operated by a boy with a laptop computer, while Clara's daughter Yuli signed energetically and expressively for the deaf members of the congregation. The pastor had explained that the "I" is a false premise. To say "I confess," "I believe," "I intend," is wrong. *'¡Solo dios!'* he bellowed with sudden emphasis. *'Si Diós quiere, si Diós intenta, si Diós crea...'* And Godo had realized in that moment, after listening to this grammatical evidence, that Pentecostalism was in fact a socialist doctrine. He knew from previous sermons that Pentecostalism flourished all over the world, and particularly in Latin American countries such as Guatemala and Honduras where the message had been carried by missionaries. But strangely they were countries where socialism had been repressed. Godo had wondered at this basic contradiction. Of course, if people were gathered in worship every evening they wouldn't have the opportunity to . . . Ah well. He'd swatted at the flies clustering on his ankle as though it were still an open wound. The instincts of creatures without a brain to speak of were quite remarkable, he'd mused.

When Godo tuned in again the pastor had moved on to the topic of Israel, 'The city of God,' he claimed. Godo had caught something about war and thought that the pastor was going to address the topic of the Israeli war against the Palestinians, of which he had read in *Granma*. Cuba of course aligned itself with the Palestinians because the USA was heavily in support of Israel and, as everyone knows, your enemy's friend is your enemy. Apart from that, Baracoans are particularly sensitive to the plight of Palestinians because they themselves are dubbed *'Palestinos'* by the sophisticated folk of La Habana who have strong opinions about the folk in *Oriente* despite, in most cases, never having ventured there. Godo had realized after listening further that the pastor spoke only of the past, and of Israel as a Biblical place. He'd closed his eyes then and drifted off.

He was woken by the piercing voices of the children's choir. Ah yes, there was Pablito in the front row, singing lustily and hopping from side to side on those big shoes as though he needed the toilet. Everyone around Godo had been wiggling their legs to keep the flies off, the entire Church a hive of perpetual motion. After the children's songs and poems came the lady pastor for a final oration and a hymn. She was a large woman and quite shapeless, Godo had noted, aside from her enormous breasts which sagged under their own weight. She'd stood with her legs apart, gripping a large microphone, and sung into it, her ecstatic face flushed with a blotchy rush of blood. *¡Gloria Diós!'* shouted the congregation, one by one raising their right hand in testimony to the existence of the Lord. And there was the idiot boy, shouting louder than any of them, drooping his head down to pick his teeth with the crucifix that hung around his neck. He was a mature man now with his mamá long since dead, but everyone called him *muchacho*, which made him grin and nod in agreement. Lord knows how he survives, Godo had thought, watching him picking away with great concentration and pleasure, prodding his gums until he'd begun to drool bloody saliva.

Godo is almost home now, rounding the corner at Museo Matachín, past the CUPET gas station, only one more street over to # 35 Raúl Cepero Bonilla where he has lived all his life and expects to live until he dies. He enters the tiny house and goes immediately to his bedroom and turns on the radio. A broad smile spreads on his face when he hears the theme music from "The Piano," a film he saw years ago at Cine Encanto — about a beautiful woman who has been struck dumb and who speaks only with her hands — small hands flashing back and forth, writing words in the air; and her child who reads those hands and translates her mother's words to the world. But her real manner of speaking is through music. She has a piano and she plays it passionately, the notes cascading with a turbulence of feeling that Godo understands and which makes him feel less alone in the world. As the music ends he continues standing, feeling the resonance in his body, tired and dusty from the street, but oh so full of the day.

He has purchased a mickey of street rum for 5 pesos cubanos and he takes it from his *bolsa* and goes with it to the corner by his front door where the coconut head of Elegguá is propped against the wall. Elegguá, King of the Santería orishas. He is the Guardian of the Crossroads, of all roads and doorways, and without His blessing nothing can proceed or succeed in the world. He is the power in the universe that allows people to move from place to place. Godo had prayed to Elegguá in the dark days, to allow him to rise from his wheelchair and move forward, to walk better and better, without a limp, to live his life with gratitude and grace. He unscrews the cap, takes a mouthful of rum and leans down with pursed lips and bulging cheeks to spray it over the empty coconut shell. He does this three times, unaware of the glistening drops of spirit that catch the fading light and create a halo around his own head. Then he smiles with a feeling of great contentment and takes a fourth swig and swallows.

∽∽∽∽

FIDEL'S SILENCE

December 31, 2014

The end of another year in Baracoa, and the streets are packed with Cubans and tourists alike, the locals parading new outfits or *segundo mano* clothing as though it were a fashion show. A stage has been set up on the boulevard and musicians are gathering there, along with teenage contestants in the Polo Montañez karaoke contest. Ángela and her old man shuffle by with their plastic sacks, rifling through the garbage cans. Eugenia's grin is broader than ever as she tugs the tourists' sleeves with her free hand, the other swollen with a bunch of *cucuruchu* cones she holds like a sweet bouquet. She has a bag of chocolate bars on her arm too, fresh from the Che Guevara factory, all the way out on the road to Mabujabu.

El manisero sits on his usual bench outside the barber shop on the boulevard. He's had a haircut and a shave for the new year. He runs his hand over the smoothness of his jaw and tosses his head proudly, feeling young and fresh after the attention of the barber's deft hands. He spots Heike across the street and waves to her. 'Godofredo!' she calls and comes hurrying across, accompanied by a leggy, booted, mini-skirted girl with partly shaven hair in a mass of coppery curls with

blonde and brown streaks. 'This is *mein Freund* Sofía,' says
Heike. '*Mucho gusto,*'says Sofía in a sleepy voice, offering her
soft brown hand. She is from '*Barthelona*' she says, on an
exchange program, studying at the university in Havana. 'But
Baracoa is a long way from La Habana,' Godo says, offering
a cone of peanuts. 'I came here to study with Osiris Rivero,'
Sofía explains. 'He is most respected in my country as an
archaeologist.' She has mulatta skin and deep brown eyes.
She could almost pass as a Cuban, Godo thinks, though there
is something slightly different about her — perhaps it is her
clothing or her gestures that mark her as a foreigner. And that
lisp of course, that Spanish lisp.

'Yesterday I travelled by jeep with Rivero on curving roads
slick with red mud, all the way to El Faro, the lighthouse.'

Godo nods, though he's never seen El Faro. It is far away,
past Cabacú and Jamal, all the way to Maisí on the south-
ern-most tip of Cuba.

'I stood on the beach and waved across the water to my papá
in Haití,' she says dramatically. 'Papá went back to his country
when I was a child.' She pulls a cigarette from a crumpled
packet and offers one to Godo. He shakes his finger, but Heike
takes one and the girls light up and blow plumes of smoke
into the night air. 'We saw cave drawings,' Sofía whispers.
'Rivero took us into a cave lit only by a flaming torch, and we
saw the drawings by that flickering light, animals and hunters
running with their weapons in pursuit of food. Imagine!' she
exclaims.

'And she saw bones too,' Heike says. 'In a clearing outside
the cave,' Sofía cuts in. 'I knelt and uncovered a patch of earth

with my fingers and I found bones, small bones, perhaps from a finger or a toe.'

The voice of the first Polo Montañez contestant crackles through the loudspeakers on either side of the improvised stage, and they all turn to watch the teenage boy singing bravely from beneath a huge sombrero, clutching his microphone in a sweaty hand, while the other contestants wait nervously on the street, shifting from foot to foot. One of them is wearing a T-shirt with the union jack emblazoned on the front.

'*¿Qué es esto?*' Sofía asks. Heike explains the contest while reaching into her purse for a twenty. '*¡Feliz Año Nuevo!*' she says to Godo, pressing the note into his hand. He cannot help himself. He embraces her with force, holding onto her, thanking her effusively before she can run after Sofía who is already dancing in the street with the gathering crowd. No need to sell tonight, he tells himself with a smile as he stashes the precious note in his *bolsa*. He finds an empty bench and sits with his arm resting along the back. Almost immediately he feels a tap on his shoulder. Yoendri Romero, he thinks even before he turns, for this is the painter's signature greeting. Romero likes to surprise his friends and he laughs as Godo turns and mimes a shocked expression. 'Closed my studio tonight,' Romero says, 'No-one buying on *Nochevieja*.' The painters of Baracoa usually work through the evening in their open-door studios so that the strolling tourists can come in and browse. Often a customer will buy simply because he's seen the painter at work and can take an original home with a story of "watching the artist create it." Romero pulls on a tiny flask and offers it to the peanut vendor. 'No no no,' Godo says, wagging his finger, 'I don't drink.' This is their ritual.

The painter drinks steadily throughout the day and, like any drinker, he enjoys company, so the offering and the refusal have become a kind of complicity between them.

'Ah, the power of silence,' the painter says, leaning back. 'What is he thinking?'

'Perhaps he's remembering all the words he's said for all these years. He's earned his silence,' the peanut vendor says. And in the silence that follows as Romero ponders his friend's reply Godo imagines Fidel lying in an old man's bed, narrow, monkish, raising a trembling finger as he opens his mouth to speak.

'No more fishing trips,' the painter says.

'No more diving into the waves,' the peanut vendor replies.

'He beat Hemingway at golf,' the painter says, dragging on a freshly lit cigarette.

'He drove the Mafia out of La Habana,' the peanut vendor says.

'It was Celia who swore to protect our girls.'

'He always listened to Celia,' Godo nods.

'It was only after she died that he began to talk about refrigerators . . . '

'Tractors, rice cookers,' the peanut vendor interjects, 'For hours on end he'd talk.'

'And we all listened, my friend,' the painter says, shouting over the ear-splitting music.

'He's made his mark,' the peanut vendor says, 'He's as grand as Hernán Cortés, Diego Velasquez, the Pope himself.'

'All reduced now, like a good soup, to this strong silence,' the painter says, taking another swig from his flask. 'But what is he thinking, my friend? Everyone in the country is sitting in front of his television asking, Where is Fidel? Why do we not see him? Why is he silent?'

'He's stopped writing his *Reflexiones* in Granma.'

'Precisely, this is my point,' says the painter. 'Is he ill? Is he dead? Is he angry?'

'He's waiting for the right moment.'

'Perhaps his mind is gone.'

Godo wags his finger. 'He's making the silence speak. With this silence he draws more attention than his brother.'

'Ah, Raúl,' the painter says, 'The little brother with the cruel streak. Our *Comandante* nurtured that weakness when he made him Commander in Chief of the Armed Forces. Remember the executions after the Revolution?'

The peanut vendor shrugs.

'No, you were too young. But tell me, Godofredo, why did he not speak when his old friend Gabriel García Márquez died? Why did he not speak when the CELAC summit convened in La Habana? When our *Tres Heroes* were released only two weeks ago? When Obama spoke? How could he remain silent through all that?'

'Perhaps he's run out of words,' Godo says ominously, and they both collapse with laughter, slapping their knees, laughing till tears run down their cheeks.

'But seriously,' Romero says, which causes them both to burst into a fresh bout of laughter. 'No, really,' he says, gasping for breath, 'This business about ending the embargo . . . ' He turns to Godo whose hands are raised in a gesture of surrender. 'No, no, my friend,' he continues, 'We want to know what's going on in the world, but believe me, the internet is full of propaganda.'

Romero knows what he's talking about. He's travelled outside, exhibiting his paintings in European galleries. He has a son living in Sweden, and one in France — places where gigantic billboards display images of voluptuous girls with moist lips, and virile young men with bulging crotches; where television and computer screens are cluttered with commercial messages in a confusion of imagery and sound that have made him feel increasingly out of control with each visit. When he comes home it is to rest his spirit in the relative quiet. Of course, Cuba is noisy too, he acknowledges as the lyrics of Polo's *Guitarra mía* blare through the overamped speakers. But it is a different quality of noise, one that does not penetrate his mind and rob him of his thoughts.

'Do we want hotel developments all along our coastline like Miami Beach? Do we want foreigners extracting our natural resources?'

Godo does not stir. He has heard these questions many times and knows them to be rhetorical.

'This is how they wage war now,' Romero continues, 'Not with guns, Godofredo, but with commerce and industry, the new weapons. Look at Sherritt!'

Godo has never seen the Canadian nickel mine in Moa, but he has heard about it from Heike, who sees it from the plane when she flies into Baracoa. 'A scar on the beautiful jungle landscape,' she'd said, *'Die rote Erde zerkratzt und verwundet!'* — that was how she had described it in a moment of passion. Godo did not understand German, but he could tell from Heike's face that Moa was a mess.

'Believe me, Godo' — Romero leans in conspiratorially — 'What the United States offers is artificial and dangerous, and our young people will embrace it in their ignorance. They don't know what it was like before the Revolution. They know only what they learn in school — José Martí's philosophy, Fidel and Che's slogans . . . ' He pauses to tip back his flask for the last drop, then pockets it and lights up a cigarette.

'We suffered more in the Special Period than we did before the Revolution,' Godo says bitterly.

'Bah! Our youth couldn't care less about the Special Period!' Romero scoffs. 'They live in the moment and they want computers, cameras, clothing and shoes, lipstick and nail polish, motorbikes, cars . . . Raúl must block this move to end the embargo before they flood us with their new weapons. How can we resist? *Es, es . . . un virus.* This is what Fidel is thinking, this is the advice he is giving his brother. Tourism? We can deal with it. We already live off tourism, the harm is done.'

Godo rests his chin on a curled fist and rocks his head back and forth, measuring and balancing Romero's words, while the painter inhales deeply on the butt of his cigarette. They've hardly noticed the people parading past them on the boulevard, spilling from bars and restaurants, until their thoughts are shattered by a sudden roar from the crowd as the winner of the Polo Montañez contest is announced and a skinny youth leaps forward to receive his prize. The crowd surges forward cheering, and balloons are released into the darkened sky as though it were already midnight. Then the shouting begins — '*¡Feliz Año Ñuevo, Feliz Año Ñuevo!*' — and Godo realizes how quickly the evening has passed. He turns to Romero and embraces him, slapping his friend on the back, which produces in Romero a coughing fit, so Godo has to smooth his back in circles until he is better. When Godo turns his attention back to the crowd he sees Heike and Sofía jumping up and down amidst the revellers, with their arms wrapped around each other, and he wonders where Heike's boyfriend Adolfo is on this, the most important night of the year.

As Godo leaves the old year behind and begins the long walk home with Romero's words echoing in his mind, he is surprised to see something propped against a pillar outside Cine Encanto. As he moves closer and bends to touch the thing he realizes it is Ángela, covered in a white filmy cloth that gives her the appearance of a shrouded corpse. Godo resists the urge to touch her in case she wakes and starts shouting at him. There is a sack at her side, its twisted neck disappearing under the shroud where it must be held tightly in her hand as she sleeps. He walks on through the deserted streets anticipating with pleasure the thought of curling up in his own bed with the accumulation of dreams and reflections that is his life. The charm of going home alone to his private room with the tiny kitchen and the crumbling *baño* out back is cut only by the poignancy of missing Marisel; or even better, a woman with whom he might have shared the riches of his inner life. But she does not exist and his sister does, so he focuses on her.

On January 3rd Godofredo climbs the hill to the cemetery with flowers for his parents' grave. He makes two annual pilgrimages, one for his father who died on this day twenty-eight years ago, and again for his mother's anniversary in

August. On his way out, after cleaning the grave and placing his flowers in a mildewed vase, he is greeted by Pablito at the cemetery gate. 'Hey, *manisero*, you want to buy a puppy?'

Godo laughs. 'What would I do with a puppy, *niño*? I'm on the street all day.'

'How about a kitten,' the boy suggests. 'We have plenty of puppies and kittens in our house.' He points to a rickety cabin overlooking the graveyard. 'Only five Cuban pesos for the best one.'

'No, *chico*, no,' Godo says. 'But I'll give you five pesos if you come to Novedades with me.' Godo has been thinking about the twenty convertible pesos that Heike gave him, and he has decided to buy a pair of shoes. Novedades is the most popular store in Baracoa and the only customers who can get in without lining up in the hot sun for half an hour are pensioners, war veterans, or anyone accompanied by a child. Pablito has had his own exciting shoe store experience and is only too happy to go with Godo. He runs into the house to put on his big running shoes for the expedition.

They make compatibly slow progress as Pablito hops along in frog mode, leaping from stone to broken stone on his haunches, skinny legs extending with each leap, while Godo limps along steadily with his characteristic gait. They are greeted by several folk they encounter on the way, as well as by occasional customers who reach into their pockets when they see *el manisero* coming.

'Do your call,' Pablito squeaks, 'You'll sell more peanuts.'

'*¡Maní maní maní!*' Godo shouts in a piercingly nasal tone which, as predicted, does bring more custom, even some people emerging from their houses to buy a handful of cones.

'*¡Maní maní maní!*' parrots Pablito, running with a sudden burst of energy down the street and back again, grinning at Godo.

When they reach Calle José Martí Godo sees that in fact there is no lineup at the door of Novedades. Of course, it's January. After Christmas and New Year the stores are always empty. No-one has money except the tourists, and in any case the shelves and freezers are virtually empty after the holiday rush. There are only bored sales girls standing around examining their nails and gossiping in the frigidly air-conditioned store. But Godo is glad of the boy's company as Pablito leads him to the back of Novedades where he'd come with his mama to purchase those big sneakers. He makes Godo sit down while he hunts for the right shoes. First he brings him a leather pair made in China with long brown laces. 'Try these, *manisero*,' he says. But Godo cannot fit his twisted right foot into a closed shoe. 'I want *chancletas*, Pablito,' he says. 'For the house?' the child asks, surprised. 'For the street,' Godo replies. 'Leather sandals, strong ones. My feet won't be able to breathe properly in those shoes.'

'Your feet can breathe!' Pablito exclaims. And he lies on the floor with his ear to Godo's feet. When Godo explains about the breathing capacity of skin, which is the largest human organ, Pablito's eyes grow bigger than ever in his solemn face. Then he skips off to hunt for sandals and comes back with a perfect pair made of sturdy brown leather, again in China, and this time Godo's foot slides in effortlessly and finds comfort there.

In the time it's taken to select his shoes the store seems to have filled up. Apparently a shipment of beer and toilet paper has arrived and all the B & B owners are there to buy, as well as a number of foreigners, some with their Cuban girls in tow. Everyone is sweating now because there's a power cut and the cold air has quickly escaped through frequent opening of the door. Godo notices as he makes his slow way to the checkout that all the prices are duplicated. Novedades used to be a "dollar" store where you had to have convertible pesos to shop, but now it seems that you can make purchases in Cuban pesos. His own price tag says 18.75 CUC (Cuban convertible pesos), and underneath is written the conversion in Cuban pesos, 456 MN (*moneda nacional*). He wonders what the government is up to now. It had been announced more than a year ago that the CUC was to be eliminated by gradually merging it with the lower value Cuban peso, but no-one understood exactly how that would work. You'd have to be an economist to understand their thinking, Romero has said. But now, standing in front of a rack of jeans in the sweltering store, Godo has a new insight. He remembers when US dollars were eliminated in November 2004 and the CUC put in its place. There had been no warning and many of the people who had hoarded US dollars lost their savings when the currency was no longer negotiable. 'It's going to be the same deal,' Godo says aloud, as he realizes that the double price tag on each pair of jeans is in fact a warning. There will be no gradual merging, he thinks. No no no! One day you will go to the bank with a handful of convertible pesos and the teller will say, this currency is no longer negotiable. And all those pesos will be gathered in at huge loss to the hoarders, and who will benefit? — the Government. Raúl's baby, *Gaviota*, the army-run tourist agency, will swallow all those *convertibles*, yes! Godo's mouth hardens and then relaxes into a grin as he realizes the perfection of it. *La Gaviota* — the seagull, a bird with a voracious appetite, a creature that will swallow anything, even the tough unwieldy starfish that it manages to digest with its strong gastric acid.

'What are you dreaming about, *manisero*?' Pablito tugs at Godo's sleeve. '*Vamos*. We have to pay for your shoes.'

Godo ambles over to join the lineup at the checkout while Pablito continues his play, hopping up and down the aisles on his haunches. It's a long wait because of the power cut which has slowed everyone down to a *más lento que la melaza* pace, and the cashier is laboriously writing out each purchase in a ledger because the cash register isn't working. Godo stands behind a *muchacha* accompanied by her elderly gringo. They have a six pack of beer and a bottle of rum as well as their share of precious toilet paper. The couple do not speak to each other. He is thin-lipped and expressionless. She is passive and emotionless, with beads of perspiration breaking out on her forehead and neck. Godo watches her in profile, a girl who is almost beautiful, but something in her is lost. He longs to bring her to life, to ignite some spark in her tired flesh which though smooth and unblemished on the surface betrays some deep misgiving. She fusses with her hair which is piled on top of her head with dark curls escaping onto her neck. She rearranges it carefully with her soft hands, the long red nails like cat's claws. Suddenly, without thinking, Godo blows on her neck, a cool stream of air through his pursed lips, and she turns, surprised for a moment before her face breaks into a smile, and Godo smiles back with a slight shrug as if to say, I couldn't help it. Just then Pablito comes leaping through the thick air and lands neatly at Godo's feet.

'¡*Manisero!*' he exclaims, 'I am your frog.'

The next time he sees Heike she's walking arm in arm with the Spanish girl. They're draped around each other in what Godo feels, with a sense of discomfort, is an overly friendly manner. He's seen the Cuban *chicas* walk like this but the foreign tourists usually have a different comportment. They should watch out, he thinks as Sofía hoists herself up onto the parapet fronting the Malecón and beckons Heike to join her. They're sitting right where the waves splash up onto the street. He glances at the ocean and sees that it is deceptively calm. He knows the sea in all its ways; how a strong wave can come rolling in from miles out and inundate the passersby. Sofía is drumming her heels against the wall, still wearing her sturdy hiking boots despite the gathering heat of mid-morning. As he draws near, Godo can see that the girls look sleepy, as though they've just woken and tumbled out into the sun to lounge like lizards on the warm stone of the parapet. He is still approaching when something stops him, some instinct to hang back and watch. Just then Sofía leans over and kisses Heike. On her mouth. Long and slow. Godo cannot believe it. He pulls back into the thick leaves of an *uva de playa* and sends a spider scuttling as his neck becomes entangled with its web. He swipes at the back of his head to remove the sticky threads, then settles in stillness to watch the girls, who are entwined but not in the way he is accustomed to seeing with couples on the streets of Baracoa. There is something soft and sensual about their draped arms and the languid movements of their necks; Heike's neck is laid upon Sofía's shoulder.

He has heard Mariela Castro on television, talking about her *Centro Nacional de Educación Sexual* and her support for *maricones*. Godo has supposed it natural that they should concern themselves with such things in La Habana where they are only 357 kilometres from Miami and therefore more or less subject to those influences. He knows a few *maricones* in Baracoa. There's Mario the hairdresser who goes to the ladies' houses to cut and dress their hair; there's Madonna who was in prison for five years after a sexual encounter with an Italian tourist; there is Jordanis who choreographs the dancers for the shows on the rooftop of La Terraza, and Pupi who teaches salsa dancing at the Casa Cultura. But women? What do you even call them? *Lesbianas,* he thinks, blushing at the very word as he unwittingly answers his own question.

What perturbs Godo is that Heike is his good friend. He is accustomed to their conversations about Adolfo and the trials of his demands and shortcomings. That is normal. That is very Cuban. He knows how to quiet it in his mind, but now he is seeing Heike in a different light and he doesn't know what to do with this knowledge. He can't sneak away without talking to her. What if she sees him turning and limping down the Malecón, though she looks so absorbed with Sofía that perhaps she wouldn't notice. He feels caught and it is an uncomfortable, slightly shameful feeling.

'Buenos días, Heike,' Godo says as he approaches impulsively. She turns to him, as though in a dream, then her whole face lights up with recognition, as though she is just coming

back from a long journey. 'Where have you been?' Godo asks. 'I haven't seen you on the street since *Año Nuevo*.'

'Sofía *und ich* . . . we have been hanging out,' she says dreamily.

'What about Adolfo?'

Sofía laughs, a hoarse, husky sound, and Heike shrugs and giggles. 'He's out of the picture. He lost his big chance for his bathroom tiles.'

Godo doesn't know what to make of this. Three years with her Cuban *bandolero*, everything for him, and now suddenly he's "out of the picture?"

'Is there a chance for me?' he quips, then blushes furiously because his own words have surprised him. Sofía looks through him without expression, but Heike laughs so much she begins to shake, slapping her shapely thighs.

'Oh, oh . . . I didn't mean . . . ' Godo begins.

'No, no, it's only a joke. I understand, Godofredo,' says Heike, jumping down from the wall to kiss his cheek. 'I will go to La Habana tomorrow with Sofía. She has classes at the university, and we will take tango lessons together at a studio on Calle Neptuno. So much more interesting than *salsa* at La Trova,' she says dismissively. 'The tango is from Argentina. Sofía has been in Argentina.' She throws her head back in Sofía's direction and reaches out to stroke her arm. 'Perhaps we will travel there together and dance in Buenos Aires, yes?' Sofía nods, smiling, pulls on her hand-rolled cigarette and throws back her head to exhale a plume of smoke.

'So you're leaving Baracoa?' Godo says.

Heike pulls a sad face and shrugs. 'I will miss you, Godofredo, but we will return one day, won't we Sofía?'

The Spanish girl's gesture is indeterminate.

'To see Rivero,' Godo reminds her.

'*Posiblemente,*' she drawls.

Godo offers a handful of peanut cones to Heike. 'For your journey,' he says.

'You are my favourite man in all of Baracoa,' Heike says, '*un caballero,*' and she throws her arms around him and kisses his cheek. Godo feels Heike's breasts pressing against his chest and he swings around as soon as she releases him, and starts limping forward to hide his confusion. When he has recovered his composure he turns to wave. '*¡Vaya bien! Que Diós te bendiga.*' But Heike doesn't hear him. She is once more entwined with Sofía.

Godo is preoccupied for the rest of the day. He does not do well with his peanut sales, and when Pablito comes leaping over on his way home from school and lands at Godo's feet, he is brusque with the boy, which he immediately regrets, but Pablito is already gone, just like Heike. Romero passes on his way to the bar for his afternoon *trago* of rum and tells Godo that Aragón is now confined to a wheelchair in his house and will be making no more trips to Spain. The thought of Spain is an uneasy one for Godo right now and he frowns. 'Yes, it is terrible news,' says Romero, mistaking the frown for sympathetic concern for their obese *Historiador de Baracoa,* 'But I heard that Rivero is coming back to Matachín to take over the museum he started all those years ago. *Justicia poética, mi amigo.* The museum is not wheelchair accessible.'

'Nothing in Cuba is wheelchair accessible, surely!' Godo exclaims angrily, remembering his own months of immobility.

Romero laughs at the joke that his friend has missed, and waves to Godo as he continues on his way to Rumbo where he props himself up at the bar every afternoon for an hour before returning to the meticulous business of painting portraits of the Santería Orishas — not the standard images like the coconut-headed Elegguá with his cowrie shell eyes, but deeply sensual portraits of real people — negroes arrayed in ceremonial robes of brilliant colours set amidst birds, animals and foliage in the kingdoms over which they rule — *curanderos*, devils, saints and saviors. As fast as Romero can paint the tourists buy, peeling the paintings off their stretchers, rolling them up inside their suitcases and flying home to show them off in Italy, Portugal, Canada, Spain, France, Sweden, England, Japan . . . Yoendri Romero is an international man and this is what he does as he paints, he travels in his imagination to each country where his works might emigrate, and his fantasies somehow invest the paintings with the power to draw those who can transport them. All they require is certification from the office of the City Clerk.

For himself Romero is having trouble obtaining a passport for his next trip, which is to Brussels where he is to have an exhibition of twenty works. There is the matter of the missing "S" on his *carné identidad* which has held up the issuance of his passport for several weeks now. While his birth certificate clearly states that his name is Yoendris Romero, his identity card says Yoendri Romero, as have all his previous passports. No-one ever noticed until a particularly vigilant clerk in the passport office detected the error during Romero's recent application for an exit visa and brought it to the attention of the powers that be. 'But I've travelled to Europe many times,'

Romero had protested. 'The missing "S" is testament only to the fact that we Cubans do not pronounce consonants unless absolutely necessary. What difference can it make?' The clerk's eyes had grown wide with horror. 'What difference? It is a difference of identity, Señor Romero. You are not the man you claim to be.'

'Of course I am, you know me, José, we were schoolboys together.'

'I do not know you by this false identity card, no no no,' José wagged his finger, 'Not until you are issued a new identity card with the correct name bearing an "S," the same as the name on your birth certificate, the original document of your existence and therefore the accurate one. Only then, with a passport to match, will you have permission to travel outside of Cuba.'

Daily visits continued, to the various offices and bureaucrats involved, of which there were many, each one shunting Romero on to the next, until he had begun to suffer the mounting tension of his imminent journey to Europe. 'I must have my passport by the end of this week, Osniel!' he had shouted finally, slapping the flat of his hand on the desk of yet another old schoolfriend. 'I'll do my best,' Osniel had said, raising his hands as though at gunpoint, 'But you know how it is, my friend. First the *carne*, then the new passport, then the exit visa. Take my advice and send the paintings ahead, just in case.'

Romero's daily rum intake has doubled during the battle of the missing "S." At first he had laughed it off and told the story at length in various bars around town. Then he'd grown uneasy and had sought out friends and acquaintances with similar names — Generation Y, he called them — Yoelvis, Yalineis, Yoanis, Yadinis, Yusleydis, Yordanis . . . there were many of them but no-one had yet encountered the problem of the missing "S" or even the additional "S" because not one of them had occasion to travel outside of Cuba. Romero has sent the paintings ahead, rolled up, certified as bona fide original Cuban works, but he feels bereft without his creations. They're accustomed to travelling together, he and his totemic Orishas. Romero has invested them with his own energy, and now he feels as though there are strings attached to his body, pulling at him as the paintings make their way to Havana by bus, to the airport, into cargo storage, onto the plane, landing in Brussels, collected by the gallery's special delivery van, and finally to the gallery itself, which is in a pristine building with long white walls where the newly stretched Orishas are to be displayed. But by now they will be wan facsimiles of their original selves, depleted of their magical energy, separated from their master, their creator, who chews his fingernails and downs another *trago* at the Rumbo bar.

Godo has to fight with himself not to go to the bus terminal next day. He knows that Heike and Sofía will be on the bus because the plane flies out of Baracoa only twice a week and Wednesday is not a flight day. He longs to see Heike one more time. He has not felt like this before, not even with Mercedes before her departure for Guantánamo. The longing is in his body and it tortures and delights him in equal measure, but when he thinks of Sofía he flushes with anger and damns her booted Spanish feet. 'A whole nation famous for their cruelty,' he mutters to himself as he paces the streets of Baracoa, missing a dozen sales opportunities. Sometimes people don't even know they're hungry, that they need a little snack, a cone of peanuts. It takes the genius of *el manisero* to plant the idea in their heads, but today he is a man obsessed, a man in love with an unavailable woman who is moving steadily away from him, from his town, out of his life perhaps forever. This is not the first time, though it is the most intense, but perhaps that has more to do with him — his maturity and the depth of his longing — than with the woman in question. He still dreams of Mercedes and wonders if she will ever come back to Baracoa. She has two grown sons, he's heard, and is beginning to show her age, but Godo wouldn't care. He'd take her anyway. For him Mercedes will always be that dark-eyed girl, standing in the doorway, twisting her exquisitely boneless fingers, sneaking glances at him under her lashes. Surely her doctor husband might go away on a medical mission to Venezuela or Bolivia or Africa — the further the better — and fall in love with a young girl there. But no, he remembers now what Romero told him — that Raúl has doubled the salaries of the *Salud Publica* workers for the very purpose of discouraging medical missions. Cuba has been losing all her doctors, Romero told him between swigs and drags. And child mortality stats have risen alarmingly due to misdiagnosis, he had said, leering ominously at Godo. 'Diagnosis! That's the one thing you can't learn in medical school. It is a matter of guidance from those who have the experience that has come with years of practice.' Godo sometimes thinks Romero a frustrated orator, especially with the rum loosening his tongue and the tobacco furring it. Ah, but all those hours of painting alone in his studio — no

wonder. One must have compassion, one must listen, Godo
decides. But who will listen to me?

Godofredo is not a man to be brought down by a thing of the
moment. He has endured too much for this and his suffering
has given him resilience. By the end of the week, though not
forgotten, Heike's departure has been accepted and forgiven,
even though it is unlikely he will ever see her again. Godo
turns his attention back to the streets and to his many loyal
customers. He watches Osiris Rivero walk by on his way to *el
Museo Matachín* with a new spring in his step. He sees Aragón
being wheeled down the boulevard by his faithful wife, his arms
too weak to manage the rolling of the large wheels himself.
Far from looking down in the mouth about his situation,
Aragón bears a beatific smile as he removes his sombrero and
gazes up into a clear blue sky. As always, he purchases three
cones and enters into conversation with Godo, informing him
that Yoendri Romero has this very day, a Sunday, left for La
Habana for his journey onward to Brussels. 'By the skin of his
teeth,' says Aragón. 'His passport and visa were issued at the
very last minute. I hope to be travelling again myself as soon
as I get out of this chair,' he says, munching on the fresh, salty
maní.

At day's end Godo finds himself staring up at the new
clock in the Church bell tower and he remembers Padre Luigi
who sent to his hometown of Bergamo for the clock, and who
was then sent home to Italy himself, as though in exchange.
Now the clock speaks for you, reminding us, Godo thinks
with a wry smile. A few stragglers are emerging after Padre
Mauricio's evening mass. Godo sits on one of the new benches

in Parque Central between Ángela, who is delving into her plastic sack of bottles and cans, and Eugenia who wears, as always, her red blouse, and is leaning back smiling with contentment. Suddenly there is a swish in the air as Pablito lands at Godo's feet. 'Aha *manisero!*' he croaks, 'I've found you. How are your new shoes fitting?'

'Well enough, well enough,' nods Godo, and he gives the boy a cone of peanuts and pats his close-cropped head. Pablito skitters away, hopping in his big shoes across the paving stones to the fountain, leaving Godo staring wistfully as he remembers that feeling from long ago, that old feeling of complete freedom when he'd been able to move without thinking, to arrive in a place as though by magic, transported by the angels. The big hand of the clock clicks into place, perfectly aligned, and the hours begin to ring, deep rich sounds resonating through the town, informing everyone that it is time to head home.

∽∿∿∽

ANOTHER WORLD

April 2016.
'I don't know how my daughters grew up so fast!'
Sonia exclaims to her mother. 'Only the other day we were
looking at their baby pictures.'

'*Sí, sí,*' says Tamara, fiddling with her hearing aid as it
whistles and screams in her deaf ear.

'Remember our little Mumu at three years old with that
gappy smile, her front teeth just coming in?'

Tamara, with her good ear angled at Sonia now, nods
enthusiastically. 'And Marielena such a big girl at five years
old, dressed in her uniform for the José Martí birthday
parade,' she says.

'Twirling her baton and stamping her white boots,' says
Sonia nostalgically. 'Ah, how innocent they were. We were the
centre of their universe, Mami. Where did they learn all *this*?'
she asks with furrowed brow, 'How to use cell phones and
computers, how to take photos with a cellular?'

Mother and daughter are sitting by the open door of
their little house on calle Ruber López. Sonia has a cup of
home-made *crema* in her hand — a mixture of milk, egg and
crushed peanuts with a tiny dash of rum. Usually it's a strong

drink, but Sonia feels cautious with so many young girls in her house. It was only at Marielena's insistence that she added *un tingüaro* from the rum bottle which had been purchased for the men — Nector and Elio, *compañeros* from work, who have helped to carry the borrowed tables and chairs from the school in front of Parque Central — and for the father and grandfather of Marielena's boyfriend Javier, a shy fifteen-year-old who can barely make eye contact with anyone except his beloved *novia*. It's a new thing, only three months, and Marielena still a week short of her *quinceanera*, but they're having the party early because Javier's grandparents will be away in La Habana next week.

Sonia watches her girls in amazement as they sit with their friends along the wall behind two long tables set up for dinner. They're snapping photos of each other with the cell phones they all seem to own except for her Mumu and Marielena who have no prospect of owning cellulars, and yet they know exactly how to use them. Mumu, barely thirteen, and still skinny despite her budding breasts, tosses her head and poses for a selfie, holding the phone at arm's length. She's known affectionately within the family as *La Doctora*, for her ambition to become a doctor or, at the very least, a lawyer. She is the leader of her school group, the winner of many awards for academic excellence, and for public speaking, dancing and singing. Sonia feels enormously proud of her little Mumu. But how did this baby of mine learn how to act like a television star? she asks herself. Marielena, her firstborn, has always held the promise of beauty, but now, with her lush hair and honey-coloured skin, her green eyes and plushy lips, she has become something of a liability Sonia fears. Just look at her!

In this past year Marielena has developed an amazing body, her hips broadening, breasts and buttocks blooming, legs stretching and curving down to her dainty feet which are now encased in a pair of very high heels. What happened? Sonia asks herself. I see her day by day but suddenly she has become a stranger to me, Mumu too, as though they have entered another world.

But the girls still inhabit the world of their family, in a humble wooden dwelling in the centre of Baracoa where they've grown up with Sonia, Tamara, and great grandmother Doña Flora who died quietly in the middle of the night eight years ago, after enduring two amputations due to diabetes. Unlike so many of their friends, Marielena and Mumu share the same father, though his appearance at their house is rare. Carlos has another family, and a wife who rules the roost, so he has to sneak away when he can and rarely contributes anything material to his daughters' household, though this afternoon he has stopped by briefly on his motorbike to deliver two cartons of *sangría* for the fiesta. '*Hay problemitas en mi casa, chica*,' he told Marielena, 'But I promise I will come later to toast you, *mi amor.*'

Sonia steps out onto the darkened street and looks up into the sky. All day rain has threatened in billowing dark clouds but has not so far fulfilled its promise. As she re-enters her house she sees it anew and is filled with pride. They have scoured and scrubbed, dusted and polished. A pair of white net curtains have been lent by a neighbour and have been hung over the broken wooden planks on the wall where the girls are sitting. Those curtains make a good background for the photos they're snapping with their phones, Sonia thinks. All those little girls suddenly transformed, tossing and fondling their hair with long manicured nails. Mumu and her best friend Violeta are the only ones who don't wear false nails, though they too have painted their fingers and toes, Mumu's in green, Violeta's in purple. Some of the girls wear dresses with plunging necklines. Look at Yanelis! Sonia remembers her as a toddler, same age as Marielena, and here she is with her breasts spilling out of a shocking pink dress which is way too tight for her. Sonia makes a mental note to speak with Esther. Perhaps she doesn't know the life her daughter is leading. After all, she's been away on a mission in Venezuela, she's out of touch. Some of the girls are more modestly attired, though they all have red-red lips, shiny with gloss. Sonia watches them plumping and preening for the camera, so absorbed with themselves, looking just like all those girls they've seen on television and on the streets, coming out of bars and nightclubs.

A mixture of *regatón* and romantic *bolero* blares at top volume from the ghetto blaster lent by Nector, the mathematics prof at the school where Sonia teaches history to pre-university students. The very month she had graduated with her master's degree in social work Raúl Castro had cut the services so that only a handful of *trabajadores sociales* could continue with their careers. After some floundering Sonia had picked herself up and got hired as a teacher. She already had years of experience coaching her own girls in Cuban history and literature, trying to instill in them the values embedded in the words of José Martí. "To educate is to free . . . Books console us, calm us, prepare us, enrich us and redeem us . . . *Encendemos el horno para que todos puedan hornear pan* — We light the oven so that everyone may bake bread . . . The first duty of a man is to think for himself . . . " She is paying for the girls to be coached in English, though they are shy to speak in a foreign language.

Tamara bustles into the kitchen to prepare the salad, lowering the volume on the ghetto blaster as she passes by, because it makes her hearing aid scream. *'¡Abuela!'* Marielena protests, *'¡Por favor!'* and immediately turns it up again. Tamara shrugs and removes her earpiece, placing it for safety in the freezer compartment of the fridge. She has heard that batteries will last longer if kept in the fridge, the colder the better. She washes her hands and begins to slice cucumbers and tomatoes very thinly, arranging them around the rims of two large platters. She chops and shreds a big cabbage, scatters a pile of it in the centre of each platter, and spreads cloths over both dishes to keep the flies off. Nector and Elio help with the cutlery, placing the borrowed knives, forks and spoons wrapped in paper napkins at each place setting on the two long tables. Plates are stacked on the counter ready for the slicing of a giant pork leg accompanied by generous servings of rice and black bean *congrí*. The borrowed glasses are lined up on the kitchen counter, polished and shining, with a backup of plastic cups. Tamara checks the pot of boiled *plátanos*, which are just right — cooked but still firm.

Finally the much-awaited boyfriend and his family arrive. Grandma enters the house like a beauty queen, in a pair of skin-tight red pants, platform heels, and a revealing white top glistening with gold sparkles. Like all Cuban women she is proud of her body, even as her well suckled breasts succumb to gravity and her voluptuous curves expand into the *salva vidas* bulging under her tight sparkly top. Behind her lurks her grandson Javier, accompanied by his smiling mamá and a handsome papá who wastes no time in kissing all the girls and downing a shot of rum before tackling the pork leg, first removing the crackly skin with a well-sharpened knife.

Sonia is in her element. She takes the mother and the grandma into the kitchen and gives them little cups of *crema*, chatting all the while. Grandpa downs a *trago* of rum and gives instructions to his son who is now sweating from the hard work of carving.

'What will you do in La Habana? Visit family?' Sonia asks the grandma.

'I'm going for a medical appointment,' she says curtly. 'What else could take us away from Baracoa to make the long journey to the capital where we feel lost?'

'*Somos Palestinos*,' her husband says gruffly. 'They treat us like *peónes* just because we're from Oriente.'

'As though we have no rights in this country,' his wife chimes in.

'But maybe our lives will improve now that Obama has shaken hands with Raúl,' Tamara says, delighted to be able to join in the conversation. Her hearing aid is working much better since its spell in the freezer.

'Agh, the only difference will be more American tourists,' the grandpa says with a dismissive wave of his hand, almost knocking over the rum bottle. 'And the reality is that very few tourists travel south of La Habana. Most of them land in Varadero and are so enchanted with the white sandy beaches, their luxury hotels, the free drinks, and the hotel staff who speak English, that they collapse and never get up until it's time for the flight home! I know. I have a cousin who works over there. No, we got our Heroes back which was what we wanted. But for the rest, we can make our own changes, thank you very much!'

'I'm with Fidel,' his son cuts in, brandishing the carving knife, 'We don't need any favours from the American Empire!'

'And they won't give us any!' the grandpa shouts. 'They won't end the embargo, and what if they did? It means nothing.' He drops his voice and hunches over wagging his finger. 'Who would we blame for the government's shortcomings if there was no official embargo? Raúl doesn't want relations with the U. S. any more than the Miami gang want to be friends with us.'

'Ah Cuba, *un nudo de contradicciones,*' Sonia says diplomatically as she watches from the corner of her eye the girls clustering around Javier and a couple more boys who have arrived to give him moral support. She notes how smoothly Marielena handles her boyfriend, seating him next to her at the head of the table, engaging him in conversation. What does she see in him? Sonia wonders. He can barely make eye contact with the adults, though he seems comfortable enough with the kids. It's not so long since Marielena herself was shy and inarticulate, so perhaps she remembers how it feels and has compassion for the boy. They're the same age, but Marielena has matured faster, her magnificent body burgeoning and carrying her on a wave of confidence into adulthood. Sonia feels a swell of pride in her daughter, in both of them. People tell her that she is a good mother, struggling to raise the girls alone, with only her own deaf mother for help. Of course, she'd had no choice. Carlos hadn't even bothered to respond to her final ultimatum. And where was he now? After promising

Marielena he'd come by. It used to hurt, the way he'd used her and abandoned her, not once, but *twice!* She'd felt so foolish, falling for him again after he'd gone back to his other woman, getting pregnant, doing it all alone, with only her mother and grandmother to help her. She would lie awake weeping quietly so as not to wake the girls and her mother — they all slept together in the little loft above the *sala*. But now she feels nothing for him. Her heart is cleared of emotional pain and she feels only pride and satisfaction in overcoming all those evenings of hunger when there was no money for dinner, when rain was leaking through the roof, when there were no costumes for the girls' school activities and she'd had to invent or borrow. No dancing shoes, no money for school notebooks, no money even for an ice-cream at *Casa Chocolate*. 'And look at them! They've turned into beautiful *señoritas* in spite of it all,' she exclaims aloud. Marielena wags a cautionary finger at her mother, embarrassed by her outburst, though Mumu takes it in stride, snapping another selfie of herself and Violeta.

Sonia realizes that good fortune is smiling on her family now, because Javier's family is as much enamoured with Marielena as he is, and they are prosperous. They run a *casa particular* for tourists, and have access to convertible currency. They have provided the pork leg for the fiesta. Marielena is always over at their house and is growing plump with the good food she consumes there. At least my daughter is safe with this timid fifteen-year-old, she thinks. Most of the girls are running around with older boys, or even with *extranjeros* — like Yanelis, with her Greek boyfriend at least thirty years old, Marielena says. What must it be like to be confronted at fifteen by the urgent desires and insistent manners of a foreigner? Sonia wants a future for Marielena, not to see her saddled with a child before she turns twenty, and then abandoned by the father.

'Time to eat!' Tamara shouts. She's turned down the music so that she can be heard. There will be two sittings. 'First the *muchachos,*' she says. 'Come on Nector, bring the drinks from the refrigerator.' The adults set to and serve plate after plate piled high with *congrí, plátanos,* sliced pork and salad, while Nector pours glasses of cola from tall plastic bottles. When they are done the plates are gathered and the remains shovelled into a bucket for the neighbour's pig, then Sonia washes the dishes ready for the adults to eat. Meanwhile the kids drift out onto the street to dance — music at top volume once again. There is no cake. Sonia could not afford both cake and ice cream, so Marielena and Mumu had decided on the latter. The ice cream parlour serves one flavor — chocolate — and no-one ever tires of it. Baracoa is famous for the growth of cacao, and for the chocolate produced at the Che Guevara factory on the road out of town.

After the final goodbyes on the street, the return of chairs and tables, the folding of the white curtains, and careful collection of all the borrowed items to be returned next day, Sonia, Tamara, Marielena and Mumu climb the wooden staircase to their sleeping loft. Tomorrow is Sunday, the girls can sleep in till 8.55 and dash out the door just in time for church at nine because Nuestra Señora de la Asunción is on Parque Central, only half a block away.

No-one is tired. The girls sit cross-legged while Sonia and Tamara lie down on the big double bed under the window, which is a rough wooden casement opening onto a partial view of Poder Popular, the Municipal Government offices on the main square. They chatter about the party, about what a marvellous time everyone has had, how delicious the food was, the music, the dancing, how wonderful Javier's family is, how much they love Marielena, how good they are to her. Then Mumu reaches under the bed for the laptop and the girls begin to work on their school project — a power point presentation about environmental issues for Earth Day. The laptop is a gift to Marielena for her *quinceanera*, not from her father who also runs a *casa particular* and could well afford it, but from Javier's papá who got it second hand from a friend who picked it up in La Habana. Immediately the sisters had begun to load it with programs, documents, power point presentations, photo albums and files of games. Sonia watches as Mumu's fingers fly back and forth over the keys — *tacketytack* — letters appearing magically, tumbling into a patterned order like a Disney cartoon. Then Marielena takes over and demonstrates a similar skill.

Even though their school curriculum includes computer instruction Sonia cannot fathom the ease with which her girls manage the digital world. It is something that cannot be explained — there are no words for how to manage a computer. 'I can show you, Mami,' Marielena says, *'Mira,'* and her fingers jab at buttons and letters, each movement causing a rearrangement of the screen, but Sonia is unable to follow. She sighs, wraps her arms around Marielena, and kisses her goodnight. *'Mi hija, mi amor,'* she says, holding the girl at arms' length, admiring her. There's a hint of something in Marielena's smile, something Sonia cannot quite identify. Is it pity? An apology? Compassion perhaps? Sonia turns to

Tamara who is holding out her arms to both the girls, unaware of anything amiss. Sonia remembers her own *quinceanera*, how she had twirled around the *sala* in her white dress, crying '*¡Mira, Mami!* Look at me, look at me!' And with the memory comes a vague feeling of unease at her own change of attitude towards her mother, something which has become entrenched as they've gradually switched roles over the years, Sonia looking after Tamara more and more, caring for her as she retreats into her deafness.

She glances up at her girls and sees Mumu leaning into Marielena, her head on her sister's shoulder as they gaze into the screen of the laptop balanced on Marielena's thighs. Sonia is surprised by the sharp prick of her tears. If I could go back, she thinks, back to my own childhood, and live my life over again, paying more attention, I wonder if I might do it differently? I wonder who I would be now, and how my daughters might see me?

P arque Central is silent. The birds are sleeping in the trees, their heads tucked under their wings, and all along the benches pinpoints of light glow as though a hundred insects rested, their wings quivering. Sensitive to the slightest vibration, they pulse in long-fingered brown hands, white-palmed black hands, honey-skinned hands with tapering fingers — each one lit up with the cellular bioluminescence of smart phones, tablets, androids — products new to Cuba, brought by family members returned from medical missions abroad, or purchased at *Los Correos* by foreign lovers eager to please their Cuban *Bellas*.

Yanelis got her device from Luciano, an Italian *viejo* she'd met walking home on the Malecón one night. All he wanted was to kiss her and touch her breasts, so she let him. He went home to his wife in Roma, but Yanelis has the tablet and she does Facetime now with Yannis, a handsome Greek she met last month at La Terraza. She blushes as she remembers how they danced, Yannis holding onto her from behind, his crotch pressed against her buttocks while she swivelled and shook her hips, as she'd been taught in Pupi's dance class on Saturday mornings all through junior school. She'd felt the swell of his *pinga* through the thin material of her pants and she'd shaken harder, faster, she couldn't help herself, it was like a fever, all the girls on the rooftop of La Terraza were doing it. She gazes now at her lover's face in Athens as she sits in the park she has known all her life, under the church clock in the centre of Baracoa. Doing Facetime is so magical and romantic. Only three weeks ago Yannis had been by her side on this very bench, on this very night — *un viernes* — his big hand clasping hers, his thigh pressing urgently against her springy mulatta skin. Now her tablet picks up the sound of his voice thousands of miles across the sky, shows her his handsome face floating in a faraway land.

Yanelis has come from Marielena's *quinceanera*. All the girls from her class were there, and a few boys too, closely watched by Marielena's mami and her *abuela*. She was so bored at the *fiesta*, just waiting for her opportunity to run to Parque Central and get online with her two-peso card. It gives her a whole hour to talk with Yannis. His name fills her mouth — Yannis — Yannis and Yanelis, their names so similar, made for each other.

The lights flicker and leap as legs cross and arms jostle on the crowded benches. Someone stands up and begins to walk, carrying the light with him. A group of girls shuffle towards the fountain, scattering then clustering as they bump into a couple of boys and exchange greetings without taking their eyes off their screens. Ángela watches them from her post outside Cine Encanto, and she smiles at the spectacle of all those lights dancing like fireflies. She's waiting for the all-clear so she can claim her bench for the night.

The church clock strikes eleven. School tomorrow. But Yanelis cannot tear herself away from Yannis' sleepy face, his eyes half-closed, that lazy smile, and those lips, oh those lips with their soft insistence, she can almost feel them. She crosses her legs and wriggles on the bench, squeezing her thighs together. It's six in the morning in Athens and Yannis never rises before ten. But he'd said to her at the airport as they'd waited for his plane to La Habana, 'Call me *any* time, my love, I'm *always* ready for you,' and he had taken her hand and discretely pressed it against his *pinga*.

'If only you were here,' she says. But at least she can hold him in her hand, a lozenge of light framing his smile. *Qué rico.* Many of her friends have cell phones, but Yanelis is the only one with a tablet. Yannis loves me so much he gave me his own,' she'd boasted to her girlfriends at the party, half believing in her own fantasy. 'It cost a lot.'

'How much?' Mumu had asked.

'I don't know. He has lots of money. He bought another one for himself at the airport in La Habana. He adores me. We're getting married.'

'But he's old,' Marielena had said, brushing her fingernails across Javier's wrist, giving him a seductive smile.

'He's a mature man,' Yanelis had replied proudly, 'Thirty years old.'

'*¡Ay caramba!*' Mumu exclaimed as she crossed her legs and snapped another selfie. And Yanelis had tossed her head defiantly. 'You're all dating *Cuban* boys,' she said. I'm the only one with a *real* man, an *extranjero*.'

Yanelis feels more grown-up than any of her girlfriends, even Marielena. Her mother has been away on a mission in

Venezuela for two years so she's learned to look after herself. Now that Mami is home she gives Yanelis money to buy clothes, to visit the *salon de belleza* and get her nails painted and her hair coloured, and best of all she's allowed to go dancing at La Terraza. She stays out as late as she wants. Mami doesn't care. And Papi? He never shows his face. He has another woman across town and he lives with *her* now. When Mami arrived from Venezuela with a brand-new washing machine, a giant TV screen, and gifts for all the family, he said, 'Fine, *I'm* leaving now. You keep the rice cooker. I've had enough of looking after your kids.' Of course he isn't her real father, but even so, he's the only father she's known since she was a baby, so what's the difference? Marielena and Mumu have an absent father too — he's their real one, but he lives with another woman. He never turned up for her *quinceanera,* but she doesn't care. She has Javier.

Yannis rolls over on his side, making Yanelis *so* wish she was there with him in his tangled bed, the sheets white against his sunburned skin, and those dark curly hairs springing at the throat of his pyjamas. 'It must be cold in Athens, *mi amor,*' she says. 'In Cuba we sleep naked, because it's *soooo* hot at night, remember?' She squirms seductively, hoping he'll notice and feel a wave of desire for her. But Yannis simply laughs and twitches his nose. 'You're a tease,' he says. 'What d'you want me to do, kiss the screen?' He puckers his lips and plants them close to his screen, then his tongue darts out like a lizard, quivering at the tip, making Yanelis jump back with a gasp. Yannis laughs at her, his strong white teeth gleaming in the light of the tablet. 'Isn't it time for you to go home to bed, little girl? I'm feeling sleepy myself,' he yawns, stretching his free arm above his head. Yanelis thought she saw something behind him — just a glimpse — as he raised his arm — hair on a pillow, or . . . but it couldn't have been, she tells herself quickly.

'*Mañana?*' she asks. 'Mmm, you can try me,' he says casually. '*Buenas noches, chica*'. Click. He's gone, just like that. She wants a declaration of undying love, something she can repeat to her girlfriends in school tomorrow. Maybe she'll stay home. She'll be tired. She can sleep until ten in the morning like Yannis. When Mamita comes to wake her she'll say she has a sore throat, maybe a cough, a touch of *la gripe*.

The fireflies are fading. One after another they disappear as time runs out and everyone's devices are extinguished, like the candles burning down in Yannis' *casa particular* that night, Yanelis thinks. They'll all be lining up in front of *Los Correos* at eight-thirty tomorrow morning to purchase another card, another dream, *otra conversación con un extranjero,* or with a friend in La Habana, Santa Clara, Las Tunas — anywhere but Baracoa with the same people saying the same old things — 'Ay chica, the pain in my legs . . . *no es fácil . . . el precio de frijoles* . . . and not a chicken leg to be found in the store . . . *¿Qué vamos a hacer?* . . . Raúl says he's going to do away with the convertible peso . . . all the prices will go up . . . how will we live?'

Yanelis is sick of it, sick of her girlfriends with their little boy *novios,* sick of her *abuela* and her mami moaning about everything, sick of her papi who never visits her. There's only Yannis. He is her hope for the future. She will ask him to send her a plane ticket. Everybody's leaving. Yalily's dad has sold his motorbike and gone to Ecuador. He keeps promising to send Yalily a ticket, but he has to wait for his residency papers. And the fat boy who sits behind Yanelis in class and kicks her desk all the time, his brother has gone to Ecuador too, and he managed to cross the border into Texas and married a Cuban-American *chica*. But I'm not going to Ecuador, Yanelis thinks, I'm going to Europe which is *way* better. But what about my passport, the visa, money for travel? It's all so complicated. Maybe if I can just get to La Habana . . . No! Yannis must come back to Baracoa and help me. It's so easy for him. He can arrange everything. I can't wait any longer, I've had enough of school, she tells herself, of Baracoa, of Cuba. She just wants to get away, to be swallowed up by the light of her tablet and fly away like a big golden firefly, to another land where she will live in the light of her own body.

That thought jolts her back to reality. It's been five weeks and four days since her last period. True, they only did it once, and Yannis said he'd been careful. He promised it would be better next time — 'No blood, no pain, just the ecstasy of love, *mi amor.*' She'd been so looking forward to that ecstasy, but he'd had to hurry back to La Habana a day early to catch his flight to Athens. Yanelis still feels cheated of her last night with him. The señora at his *casa particular* had already asked to see her *carné identidad* and had written her name in the guest book. *¡Dios mío!* What if she was a gossip? Yanelis' hand clamps over her mouth. If Mami and Abuela find out they'll kill me. And what if I'm pregnant? I must get to Athens as soon as possible so we can marry and set up house together, prepare for the baby, fill the nursery with toys and teddy bears, a crib, a stroller, tiny clothes and shoes . . .

She walks slowly along the Malecón, gazing at the waning moon that shines a pale path of light across the water. It's very calm tonight, not like the morning when the waves churn and splash, shooting spray twenty feet into the air, crashing on the sidewalk. Her belly feels heavy and swollen. She rubs it with circular motions like she saw Mami doing before her little brother was born.

'I'm just imagining things,' she says out loud. 'I couldn't be pregnant, not after one time, and without the ecstasy. That wouldn't be fair.'

When Mami wakes her for school next morning Yanelis rolls over, moaning reluctantly. She feels first the hard lump of the tablet under her pillow, only slowly becoming aware of a wet patch on her sheet. She opens her eyes, pulls back the sheet and sees blood. Then she begins to weep.